The Blind Eyes that See

Joy Medley

The Blind Eyes that See

Copyright © 2016 by Joy Medley

Kingdom Kaught Publishing LLC
Denton MD 21629 USA
Printed in the USA

ISBN 9780996404082

Library of Congress Control Number: 2016949340

Acknowledgments

I want to express my appreciation and my gratitude to my Dream Makers in my life. If it were not for you, this book would have never been published. Thank you for the push, the guidance, and the support.

Table of Contents

Prologue

The warmth of the room could not soothe the chills being sent through the spine of the trembling servant as he knelt on the cold stone floor. Thoughts of running played in his mind, but quickly vanished when he heard the chamber door open. Looking up at the torches above the throne, it appeared that the flames were laughing at his inevitable fate as the door closed. Pulling his wounded arm to his side he lowered his head as he felt his master's cape flow by him.

"I can explain my lord," the words tumbled out, "Who would have ever thought that a bezoian girl would have played such a significant role in the plan?"

With his back towards the servant the figure said, "What is her name?"

"Grace, Grace Comings, my lord," he spurted out, "She…"

"Which Zoelar realm is she from?

"The mortal one, she…"

The figure cuts him off again, "A mortal…you failed me because of a mortal girl," he said in a bone chillingly composed voice as the flames began to snake its way down the throne.

The servant pleaded for mercy upon seeing these encroaching flames.

"Mercy," the figure said as he turned to watch the flames lick off the charred body of the servant.

Chapter One

My Home

Stumbling silently over the dead carcasses that lay over the dimly lit cave, a golden-eyed boy set his sights on the pungent smelling beast. As he drew closer, the stench of the beast quickly paled in comparison to the rotting flesh that littered the cave floor. Threatening to suffocate him, the boy held his breath as he followed the deep tracks of the animal to where it slept. Leaving behind all reason, he drew his dagger and sliced off a tuff of brown fur from the two-headed creature's back.

Rapidly binding the fur with a piece of string, he placed his prize in his pocket as he turn to make his way out of the cave. Creeping through the cavern, he became momentarily distracted when he heard a girl's scream outside of the beast's domicile. At a loss to who could possibly be this deep in the woods, he lost track of his footing and fell into a pile of bones. Before he had a chance to recover the beast was quickly on its feet. As the boy tried to get up, he could hear a low rumbling creeping its way up the creature's throats as it drew back its muzzles upon seeing him. With each head snapping at him as it drew closer, the boy sighed as he was finally able to stand to his feet.

Looking at the encroaching beast he slowly knelt down to the ground and brushed his fingers across it. With a small rumble, dirt and rocks began crawling over one another until an earthen wall was formed separating him from the creature. Dusting his hand on his side, he could hear the beast pawing at the other side of the wall as he walked back to the entrance of the cave.

Once outside he became quickly intoxicated with the smell of fresh air. As he took a deep breath he heard the sound of rocks falling behind him. When he turned around, he saw the beast charging at him at a furious pace. Quickly creating a thick white fog that shrouded the creature, he took off running as fast as his feet could carry him. When he thought he was a good distance away from the cave, he looked back to see if the beast was following him. With great delight he saw that the beast was nowhere in sight. Smiling, he turned forward to see that the creature was rapidly coming at him from the front. Sliding to a stop on the ground, he swiftly encased himself in a stone structure as he felt the creature's paws beating down on the dome surface.

Seeing no other way out, he pressed his hand down on the ground and caused the earth to cave in below him. Falling into the earthen ditch, he then created a tunnel wide enough for his body to move through as he crawled under the animal. When he was sure he was a safe distance away he reemerged above ground. Peeking first out of the tunnel, he could see the creature still scratching at the stone dome. With this opportunity before him, he crept out of the tunnel and started running away – only to pause when he heard the voice of a girl yelling in the distance. Looking back at the beast he saw its ears beginning to peak as it stopped scratching at the dome. In an effort to give whoever this person was a fighting chance, the boy caused rocks to encase the legs and the necks of the beast like braces.

Running in the direction of the voice he found the source to be a young girl in strange dirty clothes. As he approached her, he watched the girl bolt from his presence in a frenzy of hysteria. On her mission to get away from him, it seemed as though she tripped over everything that her feet came across, but her determination to get up and away from him was admirable.

When he caught up to her she screamed over and over again 'Please don't hurt me,' as she tried to pull away from his grasp.

"I'm not," he said reassuringly to the trembling girl. "We must get out of this place," he said as he saw the emergence of a dust cloud quickly approaching.

Frozen in fear, the girl did not speak or move.

Contemplating her level of insanity– he finally heard her speak, "Are you an Angel?" she said.

"A what?" he answered anxiously as he looked at the approaching dust.

"Am I dead?" she added.

"You will be if you don't come with me," he said as a horrifying growl rang out causing her to jump.

Looking at the notable form of the encroaching creature – he grabbed her by the hand as he started running in the opposite direction. Tripping over every rock, stone, and branch that her feet came across the young girl's eyes began to well up with tears.

Seeing they were moving too slowly to escape the beast, he turned back to say something before noticing she was blind. Frustrated at their pace he turned quickly aside to a small cave. When they entered the cavern the boy turned to the entrance and began waving his arms in a circle. With each passing of his arms, rocks emerged from the cave walls and covered the entrance of the cave leaving them in pitch darkness. "What is…" but the boy quickly cut her off.

"Hush," the boy said lifting his finger quickly to his lips upon hearing the sound of the beast moving towards the hidden entrance. The branches on the ground broke under the weight of the beast's paws as it drew closer and closer to the entrance. There was a sound of a deep inhale as the beast placed his noses toward the hidden entrance and the clatter of its paws scratching against the stones. The beast gave a few more sniffs before the sound of it running away echoed throughout the cave.

The young boy exhaled as he lowered and removed the green hooded cape that fell unevenly across his shoulders, and rubbed his hands through his short amber hair. With a snap of his fingers he allowed a few of the rocks blocking the entrance to fall, allowing some light to re-enter the cave. He examined this strange looking girl with his burnt orange eyes. "Are you alright?" he asked as he dusted off his dirt-covered shirt and pants.

"I don't know anymore," she said dropping into a crunch position while rubbing her ankles.

"What's your name?"

"My name? My name is Grace Comings. What was that sound?" she asked never lifting her head up from her knees.

"Ohhh…that was the Varcus."

"What is a Varcus?" she said as she finally faced in his direction.

"It is a creature with a nasty temper."

"That is not what I mean. What does it look like? I never heard an animal sound like that."

Looking back again into her eyes he said, "Well, it is a two-headed creature that is covered in fur. Each head has a pair of pointed ears that it can hear you with. Each head has a pair of eyes that it can see you with. Each head has a nose that it can smell you with and each head has a mouth to eat you with. It walks on all fours…"

"Wait, wait, wait….," she said as the story of Little Red Riding Hood bubbled to the surface of her memory, "A wolf…a wolf with two heads? A Varcus is a wolf with two heads. You are not serious. Double headed wolves don't exist," Grace said becoming angry at the boy's lies.

"They do. He is just one out of thousands. Where are you from where there are no Varcus'?"

"Well, I am from Sandy Point just up the road."

"Sandy Point? No place like that exists here. You are in the realm of Geo," he said as he leaned against the wall, "You should be happy that I took that challenge to come out here or else you would have been that Varcus' dinner," he said as he touched his pocket before looking strangely at this girl, "What are you doing?"

"Since I know that I am not dead then I must be dreaming. My friend once read me a book that a girl once thought she was dreaming and she pinched herself and she woke up."

"Well, you have done that five times now."

"Then I am not dreaming," she said while rubbing her reddened skin. She looked up in his direction and puzzlingly said, "Then where am I?"

"The realm of Geo" he simply restated.

"How did I get here? I was just in the woods and now I am in a realm. You are playing games with me, sir. Just because I can't see does not mean you can toy with me," she said scornfully.

"This is the realm of Geo and you say your name is Grace Comings. I have to say, Grace Comings, you are very foolish to come to this part of the woods by yourself being that you are blind. Where is your escort?"

"You can just call me Grace and I don't need an escort. I know these woods or knew these woods better than anyone else."

"You must be joking. You nearly fell over everything in your path. I would think that you would need an escort through these woods you claim to be so familiar with."

"Don't patronize me sir!" she said becoming frustrated, "I have been traveling these woods since I was a little girl. I know or knew every tree, every rock, everything."

"You knew them well enough to trip over every single one," he muttered under his breath.

"My hearing is fine," she said, "Pray tell me…what is your name?"

"Dar Augustus."

"Is your family new to the area? Maybe you are the one that is lost."

Becoming annoyed at her stubbornness to the truth of the situation, Dar pretended to not hear her last statement, "Well. Grace. We are going to be here all night long."

"But that thing ran off. I need to leave."

"It is still out there waiting for us. It is a ploy to get us to come out. That beast is not stupid. It smelled our scent. We will leave in the morning when it is resting," he said as he picked up a rock and a leaf, "Would you like a blanket and a pillow?"

"Where are we going to get those things in this place?" replied Grace as she stared strangely at the boy.

"I can make it. I took a survivor course and I passed. I can make a rock into a pillow and a leaf into a blanket," Dar said proudly.

"You know magic?" Grace said slowly recalling another book her friend read to her as she felt her way around the cave.

"What is magic?"

"It is when you can do things with spells and potions."

"Well, there are no spells or potions. I am an Elementer. I can control the elements and therefore I can change them – well more like manipulate them. Everyone here has a special ability on some level. We are born that way."

"Ohh…please. Do you really expect for me to believe that?"

"Believe what you want. Here you go. It is a warm night, I don't think fire will be needed," he said as he handed her the objects he transformed.

"But how?" she replied as she felt the items he placed in her hands.

"You don't have to be afraid of me. I am not going to hurt you," he said as he noticed her backing away from him.

"I'm not," she said in her most convincing tone, "I just don't understand how," she added as she rubbed her eyes as she stared in his direction.

"Do you want some water?" he asked.

"Please," she replied.

Walking towards her, as she retreated slowly from him, he touched the ground and brought forth a small spring of water. Pre-warning her, he grabbed her hand and brought her to the open fountain. He watched her wash some of the dirt off her face, however, her focus was strangely on her eyes.

"Thank you," she said when she felt the water dry up.

"Still don't believe me do you?" he said.

"Not so much," she said as she squinted while looking towards him.

"It is getting late. We should get some rest for the walk back to the school tomorrow."

"A school?"

"Yes. It is not too far from here," he said as he lay down.

"I see," she said as she lay down on her blanket pretending to drift off to sleep.

When she was certain that he had fallen asleep, she slowly got up and crept around the pebble covered ground of the cave looking for the exit – only to give up moments later when she heard him stir.

Quickly sitting back down on her blanket she started covering and uncovering her eyes as she faced towards the strange boy. Not believing what was happening to her, she patted herself on the cheek several times, before vigorously rubbing her eyes. However, no matter how many times she rubbed them the one frightening fact still stood – she could see this boy as a spherical ball of light.

Trying to comprehend the impossibility of all of this, she concluded that she must be going crazy – as she stared intensely at the only thing she has ever seen in her life. Thinking back on their first encounter, she thought this boy was a demon or a ghost coming to hurt her when she saw his light approaching her. It was not until he spoke that she thought he could possibly be an angel sent to save her. But he was neither of the three. The only thing she was certain about was that he was a person. She knew that much when he grabbed her hand and when she fell into his body while they were running. Laying back down she was not sure whether she should be happy or frightened about these new turn of events in this strange place.

Nevertheless, she soon found herself drifting off to sleep, only to be awoken a few hours later, "Grace. Grace, wake up; it is time to leave."

"Just a few more minutes, Aunt Gertrude. I will get up and get to work in a minute," she replied as she rolled over.

At her comment he laughed to himself and gave her her request. He sat against the stone wall of the cave and watched her sleep for a few more minutes. He did not have a chance to see her last night very clearly, but now he could see the strange girl, whose skin appeared to never have been touched by the sun's gentle embrace unlike his own tanned skin. Her two-toned hair, golden and brown, fell across the checkered dress covered in soil. After one final look, he got up once again and shook the sleeping girl who, this time, woke up.

She rubbed her eyes and let out a shriek when she saw the bright light over her.

"What is it?" he said, rattled by her outburst.

"I apologize. Good morning Dar."

"Good morning Grace, we must go…school is about to start and I cannot be late," he replied as he looked into her ice blue eyes.

"When are you going to give up on this charade?"

"When are you going to believe?"

"Fine. What is the name of your school," she asked wiping the crust out of her eyes and the drool off her cheek.

"Helios," he replied as he walked to the stone wall and peeked out the opening he left.

"No school with that name exists," she said feeling triumphant about her knowledge.

"Not where you are from," he quickly responded as he walked back over to her.

She stood up to move out of his way as Dar picked up the pillows and blankets, and shifted them back into their original forms. He then walked back over to the wall and with one final peek he touched it causing it to crack and fall towards the ground as dust.

"There. Now we can see and feel the warmth of the sun," he said as Grace made her way over to him, grabbed his arm, and locked hers into his.

"I normally would be more hesitant on touching a stranger, but I don't want to fall. I am not familiar with these woods," she said when she felt that he did not move.

"Whatever," he finally said, "You believe me now, then."

"Not at all. Maybe I am not as familiar with these woods as I thought I was after all." She paused and then said, "Dar tell me, how old are you?"

"I am fifteen years old, and you?"

"Me?…I am fourteen."

"How long were you in the woods, before I found you?"

"I guess an hour or so," she said before asking him to describe what this place looked like, because her bruised ankles gave her a constant reminder that the roots were not below ground.

Thinking to himself where to begin or even how to begin he said, "Well there are trees everywhere which reach as high as the heavens. Sometimes I think they are so tall that they could kiss the stars in the sky at night. They are however not very close together but spread out, and the leaves and branches lay way up in the trees. The ground is covered in grass and there are not too many small animals around here, because the Varcus eats them. Some of the trees' roots stick from out the ground like a persons' elbow; as you know too well from your experience yesterday. There are many rocks embedded in the ground and the birds nest high in the trees. In Autumn it is beautiful, because the trees turn the color of a sunset," he concluded.

"It sounds beautiful. It sounds just like where I am from, but the trees seem different," she said allowing the conversation to trail off as she took in the different sounds and smells.

It seemed like silence was their third companion before she heard Dar speak again after hours of walking, "We are almost to the school. It is just over this hill."

Walking up the steep incline Grace thought it was more like a mountain, while also having the nagging thought that Sandy Point does not have any hills this steep. When they reached the top of the "hill" Dar saw Helios. The school looked like a stately castle. The walls were made out of grayish stone and there were towers at every corner of the wall. It had a wooden draw bridge that had to be crossed to get into the main campus.

"Grace, we have arrived. I will walk you to the main office to see what they want to do with you."

"I am afraid," she said as she tightened her grip on Dar's arm.

"It's nothing to be afraid of, everything will be okay. Why are you afraid now?"

"Because I am starting to believe you."

As they walked into the main building Dar described everything to her as the reality of her situation was coming to light. As they entered the office all the staff members turned to look at Grace and Dar. However, their focus was mainly on the young girl.

"Who is this that you have brought with you, Dar?" asked one of the staff members.

"Her name is Grace," he replied to the slender lady with long brown hair that matched her eyes.

The staff member stared at Grace, and asked her in a kind voice where she was from.

"I am from Sandy Point."

"And where is that at, dear?" asked the staff member as she touched her cream-colored hand to her rose-tinted lips.

"Up the road from here, I think. But I really don't know any-more," Grace said dropping her head.

"I see. Please take a seat over there, Dar, and I will get the principal."

"I have to go, Cona. I cannot stay here with this girl," he said anxiously looking around.

"Why not?"

"It's complicated."

"Go take a seat Dar," she instructed, brushing off his last comment as she pointed to two seats.

Dar in hesitation escorted Grace to the two vacant chairs in the corner. Sitting down on the floral cushion seats, Grace never let go of Dar's arm. Leaning over to her Dar said, "I forgot to tell you that this is a dormitory school."

"Why did you want to leave me?" she asked bracingly.

Lying, "I had to go to my locker before the bell rang."

"Oh…," she replied as she began processing his earlier statement, which caused her to suddenly turn to him and whisper frantically, "Dormitory school! Does that mean I am going to be separated from you? I don't know anyone else in this strange place."

"It will be okay, Grace. Everything will work out," patting her hand with a bit of vigor, "Plus, you don't know me very well either."

"There is truth in that statement, but you don't seem like a bad person."

"You don't know me yet. But please I am asking you to not tell the principal where I found you."

"Why?"

"Because I was not supposed to go into those woods. I know you don't owe me anything, but please."

"But I do. I owe you my life," she said as she heard footsteps approaching and Dar suddenly became silent.

Looking up, he saw the principal and the cream-skinned staff woman were walking their way. The principal was a lovely heavy-set woman. She had dark brown skin and her eyes were a rich chocolate brown. Her hair was thick and black, tied in a bun.

When she spoke authority rang out in her voice; "Well Grace, it is nice to meet you. Cona La'Sia told me all about you," she pointed to the staff member. "My name is Pilla Zarena. Principal Zarena I am called here or less formally Cona Zarena. Tell me once again where you are from."

"I am from Sandy Point from up the road," repeated Grace for the third time. "I see," Principal Zarena said slowly, "and when did you arrive?"

"Yesterday and Dar found me in…" but before she finished her sentence Dar gently bumped her arm off the rest. She paused for a second and remembered, "…and Dar found me somewhere and brought me here."

"Where did Dar find you dear?" the principal asked while looking at Dar whose eyes were down cast. "Well madam, I cannot say for I am blind. Whatever answer Dar gives will have to be my answer."

The principal then turned to La'Sia, "Cona La'Sia, can you please call Professor Morin here immediately?"

"Yes, Cona," replied La'Sia as she walked to the office desk and whispered in the ears of a Siphona, a small bird-like creature with lavender feathers covering its whole body with the exception of its ears which looked like little baby ears.

Within moments, the Siphona flew out of the office and it could be heard calling out for Professor Morin to report to the main office immediately.

As if fate had destined him to be there, an elderly white male, with long white hair and a white beard entered the office within a few seconds. When he saw Grace holding on to Dar's arm he said, "Ooohhh…nooo!" and started to walk back out the door.

Zarena called out to him and instructed him to go into her office, before turning her attention to the youth.

"Please wait here and I will be with you in a moment," she said to them as she turned and walked to her office. Professor Morin trailed behind her, while peering back anxiously at Grace.

Principal Zarena shut the door of the office as she turned and faced the teacher, "I saw you leave the campus the other day, Morin. Where did you go?"

"Nowhere, Cona, just to town."

"Town was it? But your direction was the opposite of the town," she said as she took her seat. "Morin, have you been traveling?" Morin shook his head no. "Morin, it is no use lying to me, because we have a bezoian girl here. How did she get here, Morin?" Morin shrugged his shoulders. "Morin, if you don't give me an answer at this moment I am going to fire you at this moment."

"I could not help myself. It has been so long since I traveled to a bezoian's realm. One hundred years to this date. It called out to me. It said 'do it, do it.'

"Morin! You know the Zoelar realms are off limits. On top of that, you know that you older Travelers leave a residue when you travel that objects can come through. And now we have a bezoian girl here. Why did you not check to see if your residue had faded?"

"Well, technically any Traveler can leave a traveler's residue, not just us older Travelers who have a difficult time in closing our..."

"Professor Morin, if you are trying to give me a lecture this is neither the time nor the place."

"I apologize, cona. I thought I did. But I guess she made it through at the moment it was fading. Please don't fire me,

Principal Zarena. I won't ever travel again," the old man said getting slowly on his knees as they cracked under his weight.

"Well, you will have to take her back to her home and to her time, and get up Morin."

"But I don't remember what time or place or world I went to," the old man said scratching his head while struggling off the floor.

"Morin! If it was not against school policies I would kill you. What are we going to do with her? How is she supposed to survive in this world? Bezoians don't have inborn gifts."

"Board her somewhere and let her go to the classes to buy some time. She looks like us, so it's not like she will stand out" simply answered Morin.

"If you have not noticed, she is blind, Morin."

"Well I didn't notice, but that is not a big deal. Let her go to all of Dar's courses with him. I traveled to a Zoelar realm in the Whispering Woods where the Varcus lives and no students are supposed to be out that way. For a time, let it be his responsibility to take care of the girl."

"And what about her sleeping arrangements? All of the rooms are full this year."

"Let her room with La'Sia. She lives on campus. Dar takes care of her during the day and La'Sia at the night."Zarena stood up from her seat and walked to the door, beckoning La'Sia into the office. As La'Sia entered she saw two smiling faces. "La'Sia," Zarena began, "Morin once again has been traveling…"

La'Sia turned quickly to Morin and said, "You went to a Zoelar realm didn't you?"

Morin nodded his head slowly.

"I knew she was a bezoian," La'Sia said proudly of herself, before chasteningly saying, "Morin you know better."

The principal coughed and cleared her throat, "And Morin does not know where she came from."

"We told you about traveling and not double-checking your residue…remember when you brought a Dragon into this realm, Professor Mo…" began La'Sia.

"La'Sia, please allow me to finish. Thank you," she pleaded. "Morin does not know where she came from and it is going to take some time to figure that out. So he made the suggestion, since all of the rooms are filled this year, to have the young girl board with you."

La'Sia started to laugh, "You must be kidding me."

"I assure you I am not."

"Why me?"

"Because you live on campus. You only have to take care of her at night. Dar has the responsibility of her during the day. I will increase your pay check if you do this for me to help with the extra expenses of this girl."

"Do I have a choice?"

"You always have a choice. But we have no one else."

"Then. Well. Sure. I will do it," said La'Sia, hesitantly.

Hearing a door open, Grace felt Dar beginning to stand up as he saw the principal waving him into the office. "Where are you going?" questioned Grace.

"The principal needs to see me," he replied slipping his arm out of hers. As he walked away she watched his light move across the room, disappearing as she heard the sound of a door closing.

Dar sat down in a chair surrounded by the three adults and knew at this point that he was in trouble.

"Dar how many times have we told you students not to go into the Whispering Woods? It is a forbidden place to students," said the principal.

"I am sorry, Principal Zarena."

"However, if it were not for your disobedience then that poor girl would have been consumed by the Varcus. So we thank you for saving her life. However, for your punishment, until we are able to find her parents, you are solely responsible for her. Whatever class you go to she goes to, she is your shadow until further noted by us. If something happens to that girl you will be punished in the most severe manner. Do you hear me Dar Augustus?"

Dar took a deep sigh.

"You are to pick her up at Cona La'Sia's home on campus and drop her off there at the end of every day. You and Cona La'Sia can work out the time on your own. At this moment I hear the bell ringing and it is time for your first class. Please go and take Grace with you," said the principal.

"But cona. I cannot take that girl," he said bitterly.

"It is not up for debate, Dar."

"I did nothing wrong to have to take her from off of your hands, because you don't know what to do with her. It may have been better for her to be consumed by the Varcus than to stay around me!" he boldly spoke back.

"Know your place Dar Augustus," the principal said firmly as the earth shook for a moment, "I let you speak out once, but I will not allow you to do so twice. Do you hear me?"

Cowed, he replied, "Forgive my outburst."

"This is out of your character, Dar," replied the principal.

"I just don't think it is a good idea for her to be around me."

"Why?" she asked curiously.

He looked down and said, "Nothing. Fine. I will take the girl with me."

"And do it with a smile. You are the first member of the H.S.A.S - Helios' Student Ambassador Society."

"Ohhhh….before you leave, Sandy Point is a place in Stone Falls," replied La'Sia.

"Is it really?" Dar said quizzingly at her blatant lie.

"Obviously, you figured out by now that she is a bezoian," Principal Zarena said.

Dar nodded his head 'yes.'

"Therefore, it is important that that vulnerability is not exploited. So, until we can get her safely back home, she is from Stone Falls.

Dar nodded his head again and left the room. He approached Grace and said, "Well Grace, you will be with me until they are able to find your parents. It is time for my first class," as he grabbed her gently by the hand. "Come, let's go."

"H.S.A.S," La'Sia said to Zarena.

"We need a cover for Dar until we can get the girl home."

"Do you think she will be alright with Dar?"

At her office door, Zarena mused as she watched the two teenagers walk into the hallway, "You know what La'Sia… I don't know, but there is no one else. We cannot keep this girl in the office all day, nor can she stay in your house all day. I pray that I made the right choice, but we will check on her later in the day. If it appears that this arrangement is not going well, we will figure something else out."

Chapter Two

Enter the Trio

In the halls everyone was looking at Dar with a strange girl in the strange clothes holding on to him. They pointed at her and some even laughed.

"Dar are people looking at me?"

He lied, "No, no one is looking at you at all…is that okay?"

"That is perfect," replied Grace with a smile.

When they reached Dar's first class, the message had already reached his teacher about the young girl and the required seating arrangements. Pointing to two empty seats at a desk by the window, the teacher instructed them to sit down as the bell rang.

At the end of the last chime the teacher said, "Welcome ladies and gentlemen the bell has sounded and you should be in your seats. I hope you had a great Shidium, but we have a lot of work to do so let's get started. I am very proud to hear that everyone passed the survivor examination two diums ago. And the top student in the class was Dar. Please give him a round of applause. While we are talking about you, Dar, please introduce your friend, since you have taken on the role of a H.S.A."

Dar stood reluctantly to his feet and said bluntly, "This is Grace Comings. She is here visiting for the semester and maybe the year. I will only be escorting her to my classes and necessary school events," he slightly grunted at the end.

Grace looked up to him and thought, 'A whole year.'

"What is a H.S.A?" a purple head girl blurted out, ignoring Dar's introduction, "I never heard of it."

"Helios' Student Ambassador," the teacher replied, "It's new."

"It seems very new," the girl said sitting back in her seat with her arms crossed as she stared at Dar and Grace.

Thanking Dar for his quick introduction, the teacher instructed the class to open their textbooks to page thirty-eight for a lesson on two of the most popular Elementers in history.

As the teacher was talking, Grace could hear two girls talking behind her. They were talking about how handsome Dar was and gave a good description of him so that she was able to picture what he might look like. But she ignored them after some time because of the excitement of being in a school for the first time. Her blindness had prevented her from ever attending any local schools. However, her mother was an excellent teacher and Grace had learned basic math and English from her.

Nevertheless, her schooling ended when her mother died because her Aunt Gertrude had little patience in teaching her. Yet, even though she knew little of what Dar's teacher was speaking about she enjoyed being in the class and listening to the students answer and question the teacher.

"Now for your homework I want you to read chapter five, and answer the first nine questions in the back of the book. You have five minutes until the bell sounds. This is your free-time."

Once the teacher finished speaking the two girls leaned forward and said together, "Hey Dar."

"Hello Aphreneea, hello Siren. How was your Shidium?"

"It was great. I missed you at the festival. Where were you?" asked Aphreneea as she pulled her violet color hair into a ponytail.

With slight laughter he looked into her emerald-tinted eyes and said, "I had to pick up Grace and it was too late. I am sorry."

The two girls looked at Grace and back at Dar, "That is okay. There are festivals always going on around here," replied Siren who differed from her sister only in the reversal of hair and eye color, and the fact that she was slightly larger than her sister, who was slender.

"Tell me Dar," Aphreneea said while positioning herself on the edge of his desk, "who are you planning to take to the solstice gala on the full moon. You know it is boys ask girls."

"I know, Aphreneea. I have not yet chosen. But I will let you know, and everyone else know when I arrive at the dance with that person," he said as he patted her cream-colored hand.

"Okay Dar," Aphreneea said while turning to Grace, "Hello Grace, I am Aphreneea; this is my sister Siren, Ren for short. It is a pleasure to meet you. Dar did not tell anyone, at all, he had a friend coming to visit him. Where are you from?"

"She is from Stone Falls," Dar quickly interjected.

"Dar please let Grace answer for herself; she is old enough isn't she," Aphreneea said looking at the fragile girl.

"Well Aphreneea I am from Stone Falls. Have you ever been there?"

"No I have not."

"Well I hear that it is beautiful and I am lucky I came from there," Grace said as the bell sounded, "I must be going. I don't want to make Dar late for his next class," she said as she took him by the hand and stood from the seat.

As Dar guided her towards the door he whispered in her ear, "I think having you around will come in more handy than I realized," as he took his escape from Aphreneea and Ren. Nevertheless, when they exited the classroom, Dar was greeted by three boys who blocked his path.

"Hey Dar, I see you made it back," the first boy of alabaster complexion said.

"I did Eres," Dar said to the tall, thin boy with silver hair that nearly shined as blue as his eyes.

"And I thought you were not going to do the dare. I thought you would be too frightened," said the second boy with the ashen skin tone. "I keep my dares, Altis," said Dar looking at the chubby boy with the pink cheeks, which closely resembled the color of the red curly hair on his head.

"And it paid off this time," Dar concluded while looking down at Grace and back at Aphreneea and Ren standing in the doorway.

"So did you bring back what we told you to bring?" a third boy said.

Dar turned around and looked at the fawn colored boy with the golden brown eyes and hair and said, "As I told Altis, Leo, I keep my dares."

"Then where is it?" demanded Leo.

Dar reached into his pocket and pulled out the tuft of brown hair, tied with a red string. "Here, take it." Dar tossed the tuft of hair to Leo.

"I can't believe you kept this dare! You went to the Varcus' dwelling place and cut a tuff of hair off of him," replied Leo catching the hair from Dar in astonishment.

"I would have given it to you guys last night, but when I left from out of the cave I tripped over a stone in the cave and I woke the thing up. I had to run for my life and I got caught out there all night long."

"Well you were foolish and careless. You kept the dare, so well done. Come on guys let's go," replied Eres as he walked coldly by Dar bumping into him.

When Grace was sure that the three boys were gone she said to Dar, "Why would you take such a dangerous dare. You could have lost your life."

"I don't know Grace to tell you the truth. I saw no harm in doing it so I did it. If I did not trip over that stupid stone, then everything would have been fine. And anyways if I did not take the dare, you would still be in the Whispering Woods."

"You are right. But that was a very dangerous dare."

"You don't know anything about this place or me. So don't judge me or my actions," he quickly replied coldly.

"I am not judging. I am stating a fact," she retorted angrily.

"Those guys are always daring me to do something. They think they are such big shots around here because they are fourth years. By doing the dares it shows them that I am not afraid to do some things and it keeps me in good standing with them. But I still don't know why they choose me. But anyways my next class is about to start and we must be going," he announced as he guided her into his next class where the teacher pointed Dar to two empty seats next to the slightly opened window. When they sat down at the desk the breeze gently moved through Grace's hair causing it to tickle her face. Her shy giggle caught Dar's attention as the next bell sounded.

Throughout the class Grace faced the window allowing the breeze to flow over her face. The sun was warm on her pale skin and she could smell the fresh flowers outside in the garden. Unknown to herself she began to sang softly. Her voice caused the teacher to cease in his teaching and the students in their studies.

She sang:

Little breeze you are my friend, come and join with me
Little breeze you are my friend, come and dance with me
Dance your little dance
Sang your little song
Little breeze you are my friend come and join with me

At a pause in the song the teacher cleared his voice and brought the class back to attention. "Now class for your homework please write a short paper on your favorite animal. It could be one from this realm or another. It will be graded on content and spelling. So do a good job. You may leave," the teacher announced at the sound of the bell.

Grace turned and faced Dar and said, "Why are you not moving? The bell has sounded; you will be late for your next class."

Dar said nothing, but just sat and watched her. "Dar please answer me. I know you are there," she said looking at his light as she stretched her hand forward.

Catching her hand he said, "I-I am sorry Grace. You are right; let's go. It is the lunch hour, so I cannot really be late."

"Really! I am so hungry. I have not eaten anything since yesterday," she said with elation as she stood to her feet, "All I ate yesterday was a bowl of porridge and strawberry jam toast."

"Young lady," the teacher called out to her, "You have a very lovely voice, but singing in my class is inappropriate."

"I am sorry, sir, I did not realize that I was singing; do forgive me."

"It is nothing to be forgiven young lady," the teacher said with a smile as he remembered the little song. "Please try out for the school choir…a voice like yours should not go unnoticed."

Grace turned to Dar as they left the class, "Was I really singing during your class?"

"Yes you were."

"Oh…dear, was everyone looking at me?" she said as her cheeks grew red.

"Yes they were."

"Oh…I am so embarrassed," she said putting her hands over her face, which were gently pulled down by Dar.

"Why are you embarrassed when you have such a wonderful gift?" he said as he thought about his mother's voice.

"Oh you misunderstand. I am not embarrassed about my voice, but I am embarrassed that I was singing during your class. I have never ever slipped into a song in public. But that breeze was speaking to me and I could not deny it a song. Back at home. I have wave friends and I sang to them all the time…and I miss them very much…so I thought to give the breeze a little song."

Dar was puzzled at Grace's speech and could only manage, "Oh…I see," before saying, "You are a strange one Grace Comings. Let's get to lunch."

As they reached the cafeteria Dar saw Cona La'Sia and Principal Zarena waiting at the door. "How has your day been going?" Principal Zarena asked Grace when they came to the door.

"It has been going wonderfully. This is my first time in school and the day has been lovely," she said jubilantly.

"And has Dar been a gentleman to you dear?" asked La'Sia.

"Completely, madam."

The principal turned to Dar and said, "My boy please go on and have lunch. We will take Grace for your lunch period."

"Principal Zarena you don't have to. She is fine with me," he replied when he looked over and saw Aphreneea and Ren waving at him.

"I know she is Dar, but Cona La'Sia and I have to speak with her."

With hesitation Dar nodded his head and walked towards the lunch line. As he walked away Grace watched his zig zagging light move through the crowd. La'Sia and Principal Zarena watched as Grace was seemingly able to follow Dar's movement, and then both looked at each other with puzzled stares.

"My dear girl, please follow me," La'Sia said as she took Grace by the hand – leaving the noisy cafeteria for the peaceful solitude of the principal's office. As they approached the office the sweet scent of hot food engulfed the ladies senses.

"Have a seat," La'Sia said as she pulled a chair out for Grace when they entered the office.

"My dear girl where are you from and what year is it?" questioned Principal Zarena as she took a seat across from her.

Grace let out a little sigh indicative of her annoyance with being asked the same thing over again, "I am from Sandy Point and the year is 1878."

"Oh sweet gracious," La'Sia said in a shock.

"What? Did I say something wrong?" Grace said a little frightened.

"No dear you did not. But obviously you know that you are not in Sandy Point any longer," said Principal Zarena. Grace nodded. "Grace you are in the realm of Geo. You are no longer in

Sandy Point. My child you are not even in your own world. You mistakenly stepped through a Traveler's residue trail which linked your world to our world."

"Will I be able to go back?"

"We don't even know what world you came from," replied Principal Zarena.

"I am from Earth."

"Grace that does not help us, for all of the worlds are one Earth, but each one is distinctly different. Your Earth is not our Earth, but in a sense your Earth is our Earth. How can I better explain it? Have you ever peeled an onion? Picture the onion as the Earth and each layer is a world. An onion has many layers, just like the Earth has many worlds. Now think if a small pipe was pushed through some of those layers connecting two of the layers together. That is what happened to you. You stepped through that little pipe called a Traveler's residue into our realm, our world. You told us the year you are from, but we have no idea what world you are from," concluded Principal Zarena.

"Will my clothes help you figure it out? Dar said I had on strange clothes," said Grace as she gently pulled at her dress.

"We will still have to look through all of the worlds to figure out which one you are from. And even then we will have to go to the time you are from. For there are many realms," said the principal.

"And about your clothes," interjected La'Sia, "we are going to have to get you new clothing to wear so that you do not stick out around here."

"You are right, Cona La'Sia. I actually have some clothing in the adjacent office she can wear, please excuse me. While I am gone, please discuss with her, her rooming arrangements,' said the principal.

"Yes cona," La'Sia said.

"Okay Grace," La'Sia said while taking her seat across from Grace, "once again my name is La'Sia Gilla and because all the dorm rooms are booked this year. You will be staying with me until we can get you home. I live on the north side of the school. It is lovely there. I live next to a small pond and there are a good number of trees in my backyard. I surprisingly have a very nice home. It is a small home, but you get to have your own room, which I think is a plus. Dar will be with you during the day and I will be with you during the night. What do you think of that?"

"Well madam, it sounds lovely and I like being near the water and trees, but do all the staff of this school live on-campus?"

"Not too many, but I moved here from my hometown of Pallarah from the southern regions of Geo.

"Is that far away?"

"Quite far."

"How big is Geo?" Grace asked.

"What you call Earth, we call Geo. For the Earth and Geo are the same, with the only differences laying in the appearance of the inhabitants and what the lands look like."

"So there are many people that live on Geo."

"A great many people," she said smiling.

"So, there are mountains, rivers, valleys, deserts, and things of the sort," Grace said, as La'Sia added, "Along with, islands, volcanoes, plains, marshes, ice fields, forest, and hills."

"Do other worlds know that Geo exist?"

"Many realms do, but a couple do not, we call those realms Zoelars and its people bezoians."

"Why don't you reveal yourself to the Zoelar realms?"

"The Zoelar realms have lost their ability to give birth to individuals with gifts. Therefore, in the past, when people like me revealed ourselves to bezoians, we were praised and worshipped as gods. Kings and Emperors alike would make statues in our honor and bow to us. We were not treated as equals, but as someone who was superior to them. We believe that, if we are to govern together, we must be seen as equal with one another - not above."

"As a result of this treatment, over time, people from this and other realms took advantage of this notion and raised themselves up. The Ministry then decided, until the Zoelar realms regained the ability to produce individuals with gifts, we would keep ourselves hidden from them. However, there are occasions where individuals reveal themselves."

"Are they punished for it?"

"It varies in the degree of severity."

"Oooohhh....I see," Grace said as she pondered a little, "You mentioned the 'Ministry,' who are they?"

"Yes, the Ministry. Huummmm....let me see.... first let's explain how Geo is sectioned – it will make it easier to understand."

"Geo has seven great Lands. Each land consists of various regions and each region consists of various provinces. Depending on the size of the province, there exists one to several Chambers committees. These Chamber committees are formed for the purpose of maintaining law and order. They are voted by the people, for the people, to represent the best interest of the people."

"Then a few of these members are selected to be on the Council board, to represent the people of that region. This is further divided, when a few members of the Council are chosen to join the Ministry, which are a group of people chosen to represent one of the seven great Lands, during summits and major meetings.

"So there isn't a single person who governs over any one province, region, or land."

"Correct, our history has shown that, that is not the best route."

"Are the laws similar between the various provinces, regions, and lands of Geo?"

"For the most part they are, but there may be little differences here and there between the provinces and regions. However, between the seven great Lands is where you will see a notable difference in the laws."

"Do these differences lead to wars across the major lands?" she questioned as she thought about her own world and it's countries.

"For the most part, everything is fine. Wars and fights do break out, but they are settled fairly quickly."

"How so?"

"Well, everyone on Geo has a special ability and when trouble arises within this realm, or trouble makes its way into this realm from other worlds, we have armies that are ready to go to war for us."

"If everyone has an ability, then how is that an advantage if war breaks out within this realm?"

"It's who has the best."

"Then who governs these armies?"

"The Ministry."

"How do they choose who goes into the army?"

"Generally, many people volunteer, but if a major war breaks out then they are pulled into service, as their abilities are required," La'Sia said.

"So depending on the land you are born in, if war breaks out between lands, you are required to fight on the behalf of that land."

"Yes, but you are also given the right to choose the land you want to fight for. All you have to do is deny your home Land and adopt the Land of your choice.

"Ohhhh….I see," Grace said as she thought on where Cona La'Sia was from, "What is Pallarah like?"

"Like many southern lands of Geo it can get very hot. I come from a desert region of Geo."

"Really!" she said as she thought about a book Julia read to her, "Does the principal come from Pallarah and live on-campus, as well?"

"No, she does not."

"She has a home off of campus?"

"Why do people come to this school?"

"There are many schools around various provinces of Geo, of course, but our school is known to be one of the best schools in all of Geo."

"So only those with wealth get into this school," Grace said bitterly.

"Not at all, only those who pass our entrance exam and show great potential are admitted into this school. This school has a history of producing great leaders."

"So these are the ones who the Ministry would pull into war."

"I would say so, but we haven't had a war in many, many decades."

"Then Cona Zarena must be a very strong person to be the principal of a school like this."

"She is very strong," La'Sia said with a little admiration, "Not just anyone is chosen to be the principal of this school. I was told that she beat out many others for this position."

"How long has she been the principal?"

"For well over two decades I believe."

"If I may ask, what is her gift?"

"She is a Curser."

"A Curser."

"She has the ability to nullify anyone's power from miles away. She is one of the few Cursers that has the ability to stretch their power that far. In addition, Cursers' powers linger on their victim for some time, as if they are cursed."

"For miles! And for a length of time!" Grace said in awe.

"Yes. Anyone within the circumference of her reach would be affected."

"That is an amazing gift! I can see why she is the principal of a school like this."

"How did she become the principal of this school?"

"I was voted in by the Council," the principal said as she walked into the room with a long beautiful pale green dress with short sleeves and a leaf pattern going around it.

"I was around 30 years-old when I obtained this position," Zarena said as she handed the dress to Grace.

"Is it hard to be voted into a position like this?"

Taking a seat she said, "This is a school that houses some of the strongest and most gifted youth of Geo, let's just say it was not an easy position to obtain."

"If I may ask, what did you have to do?"

"I cannot reveal that information," she said straight forward.

"Oooohhhh….I see. Why did you want to become a principal of a school like this," Grace inquired.

"I knew if I was to make a difference in this realm that it must start with the potential future leaders," she said simply.

"I understand," Grace said as she ended her query.

"So, Grace do you know how to put on that dress," La'Sia said breaking up the silence.

Feeling the dress, Grace shook her head, "No."

"Come, I will show you," said La'Sia as she got up and escorted Grace into the washroom to change.

"I don't have clothes like this back home," Grace said as she got undressed.

"You don't," answered Cona La'Sia as she slipped the new dress over her head and began to button up the first of twenty rose shaped buttons on the spine of the dress, "I will make sure I keep your old clothes in a safe place then. Is that okay?" Grace nodded.

"May I ask you another question?"

"You may."

"Why are you called Cona La'Sia if your name is La'Sia Gilla?"

"Ohhh…I guess I take for granted some of the terminology we use around you. It is very hard to remember what world uses what terminology. Some words between worlds overlap, whereas others don't. The term Cona, or Cono for males, is just a respectful term people place before their first or last name. It is also used to reference a person in a courteous manner. Do you understand?"

"I am not sure, but I am going to assume that it is like our miss or mister or ma'am and sir back where I am from."

"I would assume so," she replied as she hooked the last button.

When they exited the washroom they all sat down to lunch where La'Sia and Principal Zarena told her more about Geo and the importance of her keeping her home realm a secret; and Grace told them about her world and her best-friend Julia; however, she said very little about her aunt.

As the bell sounded, the ladies escorted Grace down to the cafeteria where an anxious Dar was looking out for her. When she saw the light of Dar she waved at him, which caught him and the ladies off guard. She approached Dar saying, "Look Dar, I have a new dress. Principal Zarena got it for me. Now I won't look so strange," she said smiling while turning in a circle.

The women looked at her in amazement and pondered to themselves how she knew Dar was standing before her without him speaking. Putting that thought to the side, they soon left the two youths to be alone.

"It is a lovely dress Grace. Are you ready to go?"

"I am."

"Grace, may I ask you a question?" he asked after a few moments of silence.

"Sure."

"How did you know that I was in front of you when I did not speak?"

His comment caused her to come to a sudden stop, "To tell you the honest truth I can't explain it. But I see you."

"What do you mean 'I see you?'"

"Well, I don't see you, see you, but I see a light in you. It looks like this," Grace said as she waved her hands in a circle as if tracing his light. "I saw it the day I met you in the woods. I don't see anyone else's, but I see you. Isn't that strange? You are the first person that I have ever seen in my life. Well, at least your light."

"And how do you know that it is light?"

"Because it is the opposite of the darkness I see," wisely answered Grace.

"I understand. Well Grace we have arrived at my last class of the day. This is my art course."

When they walked into the classroom they were again seated together. As the bell rang the teacher stood before the class. "Good afternoon class. I know everyone is tired from eating their lunch, but I need you to wake-up and wake-up the artist that is within. Today we will continue our course on the designing of pots. Everyone please get up from your desk and go to the pottery wheel. For power does not only exist in ones' gifts, but also in ones' creativity."

Dar leaned over to Grace and said, "You don't have to move. You can stay here."

Grace shook her head no, "I love making pots."

"Dar please get up and move to your station. The new student can have the empty one next to you," the teacher barked at them.

Dar quickly got up and took Grace with him to the pottery wheel. When she sat down she felt like she was home, for this was the first familiar thing she was acquainted with since she got here, which made her cry. Dar looked at her and took her out of the classroom.

"What is wrong Grace?"

"Oh…that pottery wheel brings back both good and bad memories. Memories of ridicule and memories of gladness. It all just hit me so hard. Please don't worry about me. I am fine, please take me back in."

Dar reluctantly took her back in and helped her sit back down at the wheel. By this time everyone around them had already started to work.

"Work away my little pot makers, work away," the teacher said happily, "And if you want to talk, talk, if you want to sing, sing, for we are free spirits to the clay in front of us."

At his comment Grace laughed and picked up some clay beside her that Dar sat down for her. As she started to mold her pot she began to sing – her angelic voice echoed throughout the art class. Some students silently cried at her song and others stopped and listened to her voice.

When her pot was finished, she ended her song and picked up a carving knife to create a design on the pot. She leaned over and said, "What do you think Dar?"

"It is beautiful Grace," he said softly. He then spoke up, "The bell is about to ring. Let's get you cleaned up."

He took a string and cut the pot from the wheel and placed it aside to be fired later. When they were all cleaned up the bell sounded.

"Well Grace, I believe this ends our day today. Now I must take you to Cona La'Sia's home."

"Oh…must you Dar. The day is still young and I still feel the sun on my skin, so I know it is not yet night time."

"I have no more classes. All I will be doing is studying for tomorrow. You will be bored, besides it is important that you get familiar with Cona La'Sia's home," Dar said as his excuses were running out.

"I know that is important, but can you walk me around the school campus. I must also get familiar with that as well. Just in case I get separated from you one day. You cannot always be my eyes."

"You are right and I understand, but I cannot do it today, but I will tomorrow…you have my promise."

"I have your promise."

"Come I will take you to the main office to see if Cona La'Sia has left yet. I think she is still there."

As they reached the main office they saw La'Sia leaving out the front door. "Cona La'Sia, please wait a moment!"

"Ohh…Dar there you are. I am so happy you are here with Grace. Are you ready to go?"

"Yes I am."

"Bye, Dar. You can pick her up from the office tomorrow. You do not have to come to my house."

"Yes cona, goodbye Grace."

"Goodbye Dar," Grace replied as they walked out the door passing Eres, Leo, and Altis on the stairs.

When Dar saw them, he stopped waving bye to Cona La'Sia and Grace and contemplated going in the opposite direction to get out the building, but he knew it was too late. They would only follow him if he did. Taking a deep inhale as he approached the boys, he heard Leo speak to him first.

"Hey Dar."

"Hello Leo."

"You know what time it is?" said Altis.

"No I do not, but I must be going," replied Dar.

"Not so fast," said Eres. "We have another dare for you. Since you so easily completed the last one, we have a slightly harder challenge for you."

"I already did your dare, Eres, and I completed the one before that as well, and the others," he said boldly. "You have not offered me a dare that I was not able to complete."

"You arrogant slug-skunk," Leo said as he stepped towards him as Eres held out his arm to stop him, "Who do you think you are?"

"I am no one," Dar shrugged his shoulders.

Eres then laughed ominously. "What's so funny?" Dar said.

"Nothing. Are you going to do our dare or not?"

"I don't have a choice on the 'not' part, as you clearly pointed out."

"That's right. Altis tell Dar what his next challenge is."

"Dar, my boy, this is your next challenge or should I say dare. Bring us each a feather from off of the tail of the Phoenix that lives on Fire Mountain."

"Fine," he said smugly, "When do you want it?"

"On the seventh moon, which is six days from now."

Dar grinned and nodded his head. "Whatever," he said as he started to walk away.

"Dar," Eres called out to him, "What is your friend's name?"

"She is not my friend. I just have to show her around school for the next few days."

"You did not answer my question."

"Her name is Grace Comings."

"Grace, huh. I notice she is blind."

"Yes and what of it," Dar said becoming a little defensive.

"I am just making an observation," he said as he turned to face La'Sia and Grace walking away.

"What are you doing?" Dar said looking towards Grace and back to Eres as he brought his hand down to his side, causing the ground underneath Grace's feet to shift.

"Why?" Dar said with a little hurt in his voice as he saw Grace hit the ground hard.

"If she is not your friend why does it matter what I do," he said as he watched Cona La'Sia rush towards the nurse's office.

"Because she is blind and helpless," he said.

"Helpless. That is a strong word for someone who attends this school – don't you think?"

"I thought this was between us."

"You did, didn't you," said Eres as he caused a gust of wind to knock Grace harder to the ground as he walked away trailed by Altis and Leo.

"Make sure you have it before the Solstice gala," said Leo.

La'Sia came back to Grace and said, "Are you sure you are alright? You took a nasty fall."

"I am alright. It felt like the ground under my feet moved," replied Grace looking downwards, "and the wind around here is strong."

"Well, I am happy that you are alright," said La'Sia as she bandaged the cuts on her knee, cheek, and arm.

"Thank you Cona La'Sia. May I ask you another question?"

"As many as you need, what is it?" she answered as she helped the young girl off the ground.

"Do you have an ability?

"Yes I do deary. I am a Shapeshifter. There are many of us that live in this village. I can change my appearance to anything as big as a mountain and anything as small as a raven-mouse."

"Does it hurt?"

"No, not really. Our bones and muscles adjust very quickly."

"That is amazing."

"Come let us go. My house is not too far, but sometimes it seems far enough on some days," she concluded as she got up and started towards her home.

Cona La'Sia was nice enough to describe the campus all the way up to her front door.

"Well Grace we are here, welcome to my home," La'Sia said unlatching a small white gate with chipping paint that opened up to a stone walkway.

With each step they took Grace counted her way to the main entrance and said softly to herself, 'Twenty-four.' When La'Sia opened her door the smell of fresh roses hit Grace so hard that she lost her breath.

"Welcome home Grace. I know you smell all of the flowers. I love flowers and this flower of the gildium is the rose. Don't they just fill the air with loveliest," La'Sia replied while taking a deep breath.

"They sure do," Grace said while holding her breath.

La'Sia looked down at Grace who suddenly started to turn red, "My dear child what is the matter?" Grace exhaled loudly and took a deep breath, "I just wanted to take in the smell." La'Sia nodded in agreement as she took one more deep breath.

Back at the school, Dar walked to the main office and demanded to see the principal.

"I am sorry Dar, but she is gone for today…is there anything I can help you with?" replied an office attendant.

"No," Dar said coldly and left the office.

Outside he saw Principal Zarena waiting for the draw bridge to be dropped. He yelled out her name until he was face to face with her.

"How may I help you Dar?" she answered when the out of breath boy reached her.

"Principal Zarena, I cannot take Grace around with me anymore. Give me a punishment for the whole year, but let someone else care for Grace during the day."

"Dar is there a reason why you cannot take Grace?"

"No cona, there is not," he lied. "I believe someone else can do a better job, like a girl. How about Aphreneea or Ren?"

"Well if there is nothing wrong, I see no point in taking away your H.S.A. membership. Grace is your responsibility. And I reiterate: if something happens to her you will get the severest punishment I can enforce at this school. Do you hear me? I will ask once again, is there something wrong?"

"No cona," he answered a second time.

"Then there is no need to move Grace. Good day Dar," the principal said as she walked over the drawbridge and out of Dar's sight.

"Grace," he said softly as he hung his head.

Grace turned quickly to look out of the door towards the school.

"Is there something wrong dear?"

"No madam," she replied turning back, "I thought I heard my name."

Looking out the door and back at Grace, she said, "Well…deary…follow me, let's get you acquainted with my home," she concluded as she took Grace by the hand. Starting from the living room she guided Grace from room to room, ending at her bedroom. "And this is your room. Your bed is right here and your desk is right here. You also have a nice window right here. Ummm…I know it is small, but…."

"But it is perfect," said Grace smiling.

"Let's go back to the kitchen. I have a snack in the kitchen for you."

"You did not have to go to all this trouble for me," said Grace as she took a seat at the kitchen table when they came downstairs.

"It is no trouble. I love to cook and there are rarely people around to eat it. Besides, I made this prior to knowing that you were coming today."

"This is so good, I never had anything like it."

"Thank you dear, my mother taught it to me. I am guessing that your mom is missing you right now back home?"

Grace abruptly stopped eating and faced the window, "No. She died two years ago."

"My dear girl, I am sorry to hear about your loss. I did not know."

"That is ok…how could you know? I miss her very much," Grace said smiling before the floral smell consumed her nostrils again, "Do you like flowers, because there are not too many in Pallarah?"

"Exactly! It was not until I came to the Northern Lands to visit my sister when I was younger that my passion for flowers was sparked.

"You have a sister?" Grace said realizing that she has just asked an already answered question.

"Ohhh…yes an older sister. I have other siblings, but I've always been closer to her than any other. How about yourself? Do you have any siblings?

Grace shook her head no. "I see," La'Sia said before she continued, "When I was younger, I came to visit my sister for one gildium and I loved the land over here so much that I vowed to return one day."

"I'm sorry, a gildium?"

"Umm….a gildium is a unit of time we used based on the revolution of the moon around Geo.

"Ohhh….ohhh….a month, a gildium means month, I understand," Grace said before she beckoned her to continue, "So you came back when you found a job?"

"Not at all, I got into a University over here and I went to school here, and here I stayed."

"Do you miss your home Land?"

"Of course I do, but this was my dream, and I believe in following your dreams," La'Sia said cheerfully, before a solemn tone set in, "Do please forgive me for asking this question and again I am sorry to hear about your mother, but how about your father, friends, is there anyone who will be missing you at this time?"

"My father died of an illness years before my mother's death, my aunt will not miss me that much at all, but I believe my friend Julia will miss me," Grace said.

"Julia?"

"She is not blood, but I call her my sister."

"Well, hopefully we will get you back before Julia misses you too much."

Chapter Three

Her Home

In Sandy Point the woods were filled with the calls of villagers and dogs. They were on the search for Grace.

Miss Gertrude Smith called the police station to tell the sheriff that Grace had run away after she was gone for two days. At the end of her call the sheriff messaged all the mighty men of the community and assembled them in the town hall within two hours.

The sheriff walked down the middle of the creaking walkway of the town hall. On his left were twenty rows of chairs stretching back and on his right were twenty rows of chairs stretching likewise. Each row contained ten chairs and all but five chairs were filled with men. When the sheriff reached the podium he turned to the crowd of men and said, "Gentlemen of Sandy Point, we have a missing girl. She has been missing for two days now."

One of the men called from the crowd, "Who is the missing girl?"

"The missing girl is Grace Comings." At the announcement of her name you could hear murmuring ring across the crowd. Another man called out, "How long has she been gone, sheriff?"

"Two days."

The same man replied, "Then why are we just assembled now!? Why were we not informed the day it happened?"

"I asked Miss Smith the same question, but she gave no answer. Regardless what day it is, the young girl is missing and we must find her. I am having the deputy sheriff make up missing person flyers at this moment, and we can go look on foot for the young girl," the sheriff said.

"Did anyone see any strange people around town over the last two days?" The crowd of men shook their heads no. However, after a few minutes Mr. Brian Gains stood up. "Sheriff my daughter Julia went to visit Grace two days ago, but she became ill and has not been up there since. She is better now. I can ask her about Grace, she is across the street with her mother. I will go and bring her in here."

"Please go and get her Mr. Gains," agreed the sheriff.

After a few minutes Julia was brought in to the crowd and all eyes were on her. Her mother, Mary Gains, was right behind her.

Her mother spoke up and said, "Sheriff, why are we rushed over here so suddenly?"

"Well Mrs. Gains, Grace Comings has gone missing and Julia was the last one to see her. We need as much information as possible."

At the sheriff's comment Julia yelled, "What?! Grace is missing. How long has she been missing, Sheriff?"

"For two days."

"Why are we just searching for her now!?" replied Julia angrily.

"I know you are upset dear, but please stay calm. I just got the call today. But let us remain focused. Do you know where Grace could have run off to?"

"We have a cave we go to on the cliff at Richmond's Point; she could have gone there. We go there so often that Grace knows the way by heart and could make it there. Maybe she went there."

"Well men, we have our first place to look. I pray that she is there. Could she be any other place Julia?"

"Not that I know of sheriff; I will show you the way," Julia said as she turned to walk out of the door.

The sheriff yelled out after her, "Julia wait! We have to get the dogs and every man his gun, just in case there is danger."

He then addressed the crowd "Men of Sandy Point, we have our mission. Go prepare and meet back here in a half hour." At the conclusion of the sheriff's sentence all the men got up and left the building.

Some of the men ran to their homes while others jumped on their horses. The town was abuzz with the news that Grace Comings was missing. Rumors started to emerge within minutes: some were saying that Miss Smith probably ran that girl out the house; others said Grace had run away with the gypsies; yet others said she is probably home in bed asleep.

Nevertheless within thirty minutes the men were back and heading off to Richmond's Point. When they got close to the cave Julia took off running, yelling Grace's name, hoping to see her dear friend sitting on her favorite stone. But when she reached the cave there was no sign of Grace. Julia fell down to the ground and started to cry, for she really believed that Grace came to this place. Through a stream of tears she said, "Sheriff, I thought she would be here. What if she has been eaten by a bear or a wolf or a wild dog?"

Julia's mother came up behind her, put her arms around her daughter, and looked up at the sheriff who said, "I don't believe she is dead. If she was eaten there would be blood and bones here and there are none." The sheriff then turned to the men and said, "Men she is not here. Check the surrounding woods. We have five hours before nightfall; do all the searching you can within that amount of time."

Immediately all the men dispersed out and you could hear "Grace!" echoing throughout the woods, mingling with the sound of dogs barking. The men searched for hours. However, no one found any trace of Grace anywhere. After sitting in the cave with her mother for several hours Julia got up to leave. She and her mother were walking down the winding path that lead to the cave when Julia looked down and saw a metal object glistening in the sun. When she came closer she saw that it was the charm bracelet she gave Grace two days ago. She picked it up and just looked at it. She looked at it so long that the silence scared her mother.

"Julia what is the matter?" With tear-filled eyes she looked up at her mother and then at the sheriff approaching her and said, "This is the bracelet I gave to Grace when I last saw her. I told you she would come up this way and that she knew her way here. But now she is gone."

The sheriff sent a messenger boy to run throughout the woods informing all the men they could return for the day. When all of the men gathered around the sheriff he told them about Julia's find and suggested that everyone return to their homes for the night. But one man called out, "What if someone grabbed her as she was coming to the cave, Sheriff?"

He simply replied, "Then there is nothing we can do about it in the woods. If we got the call earlier then we may have been able to chase the person down, but after two days. . . I believe his or her trail is cold. I hate to say it, but let's shut it down today. Please go home with your family and send a prayer to God for the safety of this child."

As everyone was walking down the path, Julia looked back and tears started to roll down her face. She said, "Jesus, wherever Grace is please keep her safe."

Back in the realm of Geo, Grace went up to her room and got in bed. Her last thought as Cona La'Sia blew out the candle was 'This is much more comfortable then sleeping on the ground.' Suddenly she climbed out of bed and got on her knees and said, "Lord Jesus, thank you for your hedge of protection yesterday and not letting me be eaten by that wolf-thing. Also thank you for Dar and please don't let Julia worry too much about me while I am gone, Amen." At the end of her prayer she got up and climbed into bed and fell asleep.

Chapter Four

The Plan

Early the next morning Grace heard a loud crash outside of her door. She got up quickly and went to the door. When she walked out she tripped over something lying in the floor. Hitting the ground she suddenly heard La'Sia laughing next to her, who was lying flat down on the ground covered with Grace's breakfast. While laughing La'Sia said, "I am grateful that I am still in my night clothes."

The two of them sat on the floor for the next few minutes and laughed while La'Sia told Grace what happened, as she picked food out of her hair.

"I am sorry, Grace, about the food, and there is not enough time for me to make any more."

"Don't worry about it, Cona La'Sia. I am not that hungry anyways. I am just excited to get to school and listen to all of Dar's classes."

"You had a good time yesterday."

"I did."

Grace reached down to touch her wrist and noticed that her bracelet was missing. She felt on the floor. "What are you looking for dear?"

"My bracelet; it is not on my wrist."

"Well it is not on the floor dear. And I did not see it on your wrist all of yesterday."

"My friend gave me that bracelet and now it is gone, maybe it is in that place I was at when I stepped through the Traveler's residue."

"Well if it is there dear, it is too dangerous to go searching for it."

"I know, but I am sure she will be upset."

"I believe she will understand. Now you need to get washed up and dressed, for school is about to start soon," she said while handing Grace a bowl of water with a washcloth. "Dear, your clothes are on your bed. I will be up in fifteen minutes to get you. Do you need help getting dressed again?"

"No I do not, but thank you for asking," replied Grace. She then asked, "La'Sia, what color is my dress today?"

"It is like the color of a sunset. I will say it is burnt orange."

"Like Dar's eyes."

"Yes. How did you know Dar's eyes were that color?"

"I overheard some girls talking about him."

"I see. Okay, go wash up and get dressed. I will be up shortly." When she shut the door Grace quickly undressed and started to wash.

After she washed and got dressed she sat down on the bed and waited for La'Sia to come and get her. However, impatience overcame her and she went to the window and let the shine beams dance across her face. After a few minutes she heard a knock at the door.

"Are you ready dear? It is time to go."

La'Sia guided Grace down the stairs and out the front door. She counted her steps from the front door to the gate entrance and it was twenty-four steps, just as before.

They had a seemingly quiet but nice walk to the main school building. When they walked into the main office Dar was waiting for Grace. However, before La'Sia could tell Grace Dar was there Grace turned to her and said, "Thank you, I will meet you this evening," and she walked over to Dar, only bumping into one chair on her mission to that bright white light.

"Good morning Dar," Grace said cheerfully, but Dar responded with a cold "Good morning."

"What is wrong Dar? You do not seem yourself," replied Grace still trying to be cheerful.

"So, now you know me so well after just one and a half days. Please, you do not know me well enough to judge whether I am myself or not. Let's go," Dar said pulling Grace by her bicep.

Dar was not the person she remembered him to be yesterday. He was cold and standoffish to her. He would not speak to her and when she asked him a question he would give her a very brief and incomplete answer. She thought to herself 'maybe this was the real Dar.'

After his first two classes were finished he said to Grace, "I guess I got to feed you now."

At this point her cheerfulness broke, "I am not a dog that you have to take care of! You are a rude and nasty boy and I hate you! If this is the real you I am disgusted by you!" she said as she pulled her arm from his grip.

She started to walk away when she heard Dar speaking to her. "I told you when we first met in the woods that you did not know me. Now you do. I am a loner. I don't want to care for or babysit anyone. Especially a blind girl who I do not know. What made you think we were friends or even could be friends? You think spending one day with me makes us comrades? You know nothing, Grace. It is best this way."

At the end of his words, as the bell rung, she walked away, bumping into many people on her quest to get away from him. Dar watched her walk away, joyful his plan had succeeded. He thought, 'Now the principal will assign her to someone else.'

When he turned to go to the cafeteria his second period teacher was standing behind him looking at him through his silvery blue eyes. "Oh…Professor Lynos you scared me." Professor Lynos did not say a word, but he just looked towards Grace struggling to go down the hallway with her arms outstretched. He then looked down at Dar again and said, "I am disappointed at you Dar. I did not think you were one of those guys who could be easily intimidated."

"But Professor you don't understand…" he said to the gentleman with the snowy white hair that only darkened at his temples.

"I understand more than you think I do. Let me tell you something. Saving someone is not hurting that person you are trying to save. It would have been better to tell her the truth than to make her feel unwanted – especially since she is so far from home."

"You know where Grace is from Professor?"

"No I do not know where she is from. I know where she is not from," Professor Lynos said as he took a step towards Grace who was knocked down to the floor by a student. He watched Grace crawl to the wall where she brought her knees to her chest and cried.

"It is best this way," he said turning from his professor and walking towards the cafeteria.

"Is it?!" he yelled after him.

"It has to be. There is no other way that I can think of!"

"Then you are not as mature as I once thought you to be Dar Augustus."

"I guess not."

"I understand. At least help her to the office," the professor said as he went back into his classroom.

Dar then turned and walked slowly over to Grace. When she saw him coming she quickly got up and stayed close to the wall, trying to run away as she felt her way down the hallway. At this point, all of the students were out of the hallway, making it easy for Dar to catch up to her.

Grace turned to him and said, "What do you want Dar? Do you feel sorry for this poor dog that you have to take care of? Well don't. I don't need you and I don't need anyone. I only have two true friends and you are not one. You are a wicked wretch hurtful hateful boy and I don't like you at all."

"I came to help you to the office, that is all" he said as he reached out to touch her arm, which caused her to scream, a scream unlike any he had ever heard before. It was filled with so much hurt that for a moment he thought he heard the earth gasp.

"Grace," Dar mustered when he saw the principal coming down the hallway.

"Grace what is the matter?" the principal asked when she arrived.

"I think I want to go home now. I don't feel well."

"But Cona La'Sia told me you were doing so well this morning and that you were excited to be in school today."

"I don't know; I just feel ill."

"Well I will have Dar take you back to Cona La'Sia's home."

But Grace quickly said, "No, I can wait in the office until the end of the day."

"If that is your choice, then come with me. Dar, you may go to lunch now," she said as she walked Grace to the office.

Walking to the lunch door he was greeted by Eres and his crew. "Man, you are cold Dar, I did not think you had it in you to treat your friend like that," Altis said while putting his arm around his shoulder.

Dar laughed and said, "I told you she was not my friend, just a girl that I had to go around with. I guess I am kicked out of the H.S.A.S."

Chapter Five

Why Me?

At the end of the day, Dar sat on the stonewall and watched Cona La'Sia and Grace walk away. A smile crept across his face knowing his plan had succeeded. However, it was quickly washed away as he watched his classmates pass him by with an occasional nod or a goodbye – but only the type that you would give any stranger to be polite.

Nevertheless, in his own way, Dar was proud that he had trained everyone not to ask him to go places with them anymore, with the exception of Aphreneea and Ren who just refused to catch the hints, no matter what he did. As he watched the last people walk away he hopped down from the short wall and walked to his dorm room, his four-walled prison. Yet, this room was the only safe haven he had from the world - the world that he could no longer be a part of.

"How? How did I get to be this person?" he thought to himself as he lay back on his bed, allowing the silence to bang at his ears. "How?" he murmured recalling his first days at the school.

"Just because you made your way to this campus does not mean that you are admitted to this school," an instructor barked at the potential incoming class, "Look around you, many of you will not make it into this school, as you are too weak to overcome the trials ahead of you. You will have three days and three days only to show us your worth."

"This is Professor Morin," the instructor pointed to a very old man with long white hair, a white beard, and pale colored skin that hung loosely from his fragile boney body, "He will be monitoring your Travelers today," he announced as he pointed to twenty individuals with a diamond shape birth mark on their forehead, "These individuals will be transporting you to your various testing locations. If you see one of them during your trials then you know that you have succeeded. If you do not see one of them within one hour then you have failed. We start now!" the instructor said as the old man instructed the Travelers to open their rips, as Dar suddenly found himself in a desert setting.

'Am I even on Geo?' Dar thought to himself as he stood alone in the middle of a sea of sandy dunes as far as the eye can see. "At least they could have told us what to do," he said sighing as he looked to the north, south, east, and west as the sun beat down on him.

Taking a deep breath, Dar formed a small cloud over his head to block the sun, before reaching down to pick up a hand full of sand. Grinding his hands together, he fashioned the sand into the shape of an arrow.

Closing his eyes he launched it up into the sky with a funnel of air as its guide. He decided that he would allow fate to choose which direction he should go. When he heard the arrow hit the ground, he looked down to see that he would be heading northward.

Feeling the heat of the desert, Dar allowed a gentle rainfall to emerge from the cloud he formed before he headed out. However, before he could take two steps the ground beneath him opened up and he began falling into an open chasm. To stop his decent, he created a gust of wind to propel him towards one of many ivory colored spikes protruding from the walls.

When he reached the wall, he looked up to notice that the opening of the chasm was beginning to close. Without thinking twice, he broke off one of the ivory spikes, which caused a deafening roar to emerge out of the depth of the chasm, followed by a putrid gust of air that nearly knocked him from the wall.

It was at this moment that Dar realized that he was in the jaws of a Desert Worm and he had just broken off one of its teeth. Quickly placing the tooth under his arm, he swirled his free hand in the air to create a massive storm cloud - as the old desert proverb about these worms bubbled to the surface of his memory:

Desert travelers take warning, when the skies get stormy
Desert travelers' delight, when there's no cloud in sight.

As the rain water poured down the creatures' throat, Dar could see that the mouth of the creature began to open wider. Moving quickly, Dar transform the broken tooth into an elastic band that he attached to one side of an angled tooth and to the other side of an angled tooth on the opposite side of the creatures mouth.

Positioning himself in the middle of this elastic band, he shot a powerful funnel of air uppers, causing the elastic band to rapidly be propelled downwards. When he thought he had enough downward force, Dar closed up his hands, causing the air funnel to cease, which cause the elastic band to rebound, giving him an upward thrust as he was shot out of the creatures mouth like an arrow from a bow.

Flying out of the creature's mouth, Dar was immediately pulled into a Traveler's rip, where he slid face forward in front of the instructor's feet.

"Well, I guess this means you have completed Day 1," the instructor said as he walked away.

Faced down in the dirt, Dar just nodded his head, before rolling over onto his back to see more candidates calmly walking through different openings. Looking up, Dar noticed a shadow slowly creeping its way towards him, until it settled above him. Glancing upward a little more, he watched as the old Traveler stared down at him before inquiring, "Are you a Traveler?"

Too sore to move, "No, cono, I am an Elementer."

"Interesting that you would be the only one to end up so far outside the testing parameters," he said as he placed his hands behind his back and walked away.

'Outside of the testing parameters,' Dar thought as he was finally able to roll over and get off of the ground.

Looking at the number of candidates left, he estimated that well over half of the people failed.

"That was intense," one of the candidates said.

"Yeah! It was. If you don't understand your gifts, it would have been impossible for you to do everything they asked you to do."

"Wait?! What?" Dar said bulging in on their conversation, "What did you have to do?"

"Just like everyone. We had to show third level of mastery of our gift," she answered with a puzzled look on her face.

"How did you show your mastery?" Dar questioned.

"When I arrived at my site there was a package waiting for me that listed ten things I had to do in a set amount of time. I expected them to ask me to perform complex things, but the extent of it, I could not have imagined," she said looking at the other candidate who nodded his head.

"Was your list hard?" she was saying when she looked up to see that Dar had walked away.

Confused, but now understanding Professor Morin earlier statement, his attention was drawn back when the instructor announced that Day 1 testing was over and everyone was going to get their room assignments.

"This is a lucky class. Everyone gets their own room this year, since the other candidates failed to complete their first test," he concluded as he gave out the keys.

When everyone departed for their room, Dar thought he found his room really quickly. He went in and immediately fell asleep across his bed but, was soon awoken by a knock at the door. When he opened the door, he looked up to see a new instructor announcing that Day 2 was about to begin.

Looking out of the window, Dar did not feel like he slept through the whole day, but obviously he did, as he was guided out of the dormitory. "Where are the others?" he inquired.

"They have already been taken. You are the last one."

Nodding his head to acknowledge that he understood, Dar was lead to an open field. Looking around, he was about to ask the instructor a question, when he noticed that he was alone. Sighing he thought, 'Day 2.'

Hearing rustling in the adjust woods, he braced himself for the next assignment when he saw Professor Morin emerge, "Well, well, well….I did not lose track of you this time young lad," the Professor said as he stroked his beard, "I thought I sensed something strange," he concluded as he waved for Dar to follow him, "You aren't on campus right now, boy."

Stepping through a Traveler's rip Dar reemerged to find himself surrounded by the instructor from the morning and a woman with deep rich brown skin that matched her eyes. With her thick ebony hair, pulled into a stylish bun she said to Dar, "Well, this has been a busy, busy year during testing time for this one."

Looking at the curvy woman, with full lips Dar was about to ask her a question when she gave him a directive to follow her. Leading him away, she introduced herself as the principal of the school. Peering behind him, he watched as Professor Morin attempted to keep up.

Nearly crashing into her when he looked forward, she pointed him in the direction of his dormitory and said, "Please return to your room."

When walking away, he heard her give instructions to the staff to be extra vigilant of the candidates.

As Day 2 advanced, a second instructor introduced herself to the group of candidates. She noted that this day was more academic based than that of displaying abilities. Beckoning the candidates to follow her, she led them to their testing locations.

When they arrived, each candidate was positioned one seat apart from one another. As Dar took his seat, he surveyed the room with its high cathedral wall made of various shades of grey stones. His eyes were drawn to the wooden beams that straddled the room as they stretched from left to right and down to the glass windows that stretched from floor to ceiling that were covered in intricate metal workings.

His attention was drawn back, when the test was placed in front of him with a writing utensil. The instructor announced the time duration and rules for the test, before allowing them to begin.

By the end of the test, Dar thought that it was fairly easy. He felt knowledgeable about the various gifts, people, and regions of Geo. He especially knew that he shined on the Elementer portion of the test, although there were a few questions that he knew that he got wrong, but for the most part he felt confident.

While waiting for the testing session to come to an end, he looked around the room and watched as several other candidates tried to feverishly finish the test as time was ticking down. When time was called, Dar heard audible groanings, as some candidates did not reach the end of the test.

Leaving the test location, they were immediately led to the lunch hall where they would await their results. Many of the candidates could not eat, as they were too nervous to hold down any food; while others tried to eat with the disastrous results of it violently coming back up.

Dar and a few other candidates seem to migrate towards each other, as they did not have any trouble eating. "What did you think of the test?" one candidate asked aloud as he put a spoonful of soup in his mouth.

"Wasn't as bad as I thought it was going to be," another candidate cockily answered.

"Do you think Day 3 will be hard?" someone said looking at Dar.

"Do you think you are good enough to pass Day 3?" Dar replied as he took a spoonful of soup.

"Of course," he replied.

"Then it doesn't matter, because you should have the confidence to know that you are going to pass," he said directly.

"True," the candidate replied as he nodded his head slowly, "true," he said again as he let the conversation merge into what they do on a normal day.

An hour passed before Dar and the other candidates finally heard the doors to the lunch hall open. Standing in the doorway was the test examiner with the results in her hand. She announced that as each name was called, they should immediately leave the premise, for they did not achieve the score needed to pass Day 2.

As each name was called, the number of candidates dwindled further and further down until the last name was called.

Smiling at Dar, a candidate said to him, "I guess I don't have to worry about Day 3 after all," he said as he got up to leave.

Scanning the room, Dar estimated that about 30% of the candidates remained from before.

"Tomorrow is the last day, if you pass tomorrow's exam you will official become a student of Helios," the instructor said as she allowed the candidates to disperse for the day.

The next day, came the quickest in Dar opinion as he found himself positioned across from several of the previous instructors and the principal he had met earlier.

Sitting in the hard wooden chair facing the row of adults sitting behind a long wooden table, he braced himself for an onslaught of questions. For Day 3 was announced to be a formal interview day.

Taking a deep breath when he heard the first question asked, he relayed his answers with as much eloquence as he could muster - as one question came after another. After 45 minutes of endless questions of: Where do you see yourself in the future? What can you bring to Helios? Who inspires you the most? Why should we choose you? He was released to the waiting room with the other candidates previously interviewed.

Looking around the room, he noticed that the waiting location was an antique looking library - that had books stretching from the ceiling to the floor. It had a similar design like that of the testing room, but a calmer feel to it.

Taking a seat on a cushion sofa, Dar kicked up his legs and laid back as he allowed his ears to ease drop on the various conversations around the room. He noticed, after some time, that each candidate's interview was a different amount of time as the day moved forward. The longer interviews were first and the shorter interviews were towards the end. By the time the last candidate finished, the sun gave way to the moon's gentle glow.

Following the last candidate's entrance, an instructor entered telling everyone that they could go to their rooms for the evening. Those who passed would find a gold envelope under their door the following morning.

Hearing a knock at the door, Dar broke from reminiscing about his past, when his neighbor inquired about a homework assignment due the following day. Attempting to keep the conversation as short as possible he wrote it down on a piece of paper and handed it to him.

Shutting the door, he slid down the backside of it to the floor. As he pulled his knees to his chest he allowed his mind to drift to the first day of classes at Helios.

"Hello everyone, my name is Dar Augustus," he announced to the class as the teacher called on him to stand.

"Where are you from Dar?" the teacher asked.

"All around sir, I don't really have a place I would call home."

"Is there anything else you want us to know about you?"

Shaking his head, no, the instructor said, "Okay, take your seat. Next."

Dar listened to everyone as they announced their names and where they lived and what they liked to do on their free time. However, one student in particular caught his attention when the teacher asked him why he was in this course when he was a third year.

"I just find this course fascinating, cono, and a recap never hurt anyone," a handsome, fair skinned boy said

"But you do not need this course. There must be another course that would be more appropriate for your level, Eres," the teacher said with a bit of trepidation in his voice.

"I am happy in this course, cono, and I have the room in my schedule," he said as a bit of annoyance crept into his voice, his insubordination causing the teacher to become unnerved.

"Please stand and introduce yourself."

His silver hair seemed to shine as blue as his eyes. His smooth voice had all the girls on the edge of their seats and all the guys wishing they were him – if not just for a moment. After his introduction he took his seat, made eye contact with Dar, and smiled, which sent eerie shivers down Dar's spine. Dar wanted to look away but it seemed this Eres had a hold on him. It was not until the teacher clapped his hands that the connection was broken.

At the end of class Dar left quickly from the classroom to make his way to his next class, only to get lost. When he turned around to retrace his steps Eres was standing behind him, staring at him with those crystal blue eyes.

"So you are Dar Augustus, right?" he said looking down at the boy.

"I am."

"Well, I am…."

"Eres," Dar finished his sentence.

"I am, nice memory."

"What can I do for you, Eres?"

"It looks like you are lost. I just came to offer my assistance to you. Which class are you going to now?" he said as he took Dar's schedule from his hand.

"Introduction to the Elements."

"So you are an Elementer, are you not?"

"I am."

"Me too. If you ever need any help in that course, just ask."

Dar nodded his head in agreement, but something about his tone made him decide that he would never take him up on his offer.

"Here you go. The class is right over there. This is a really nice teacher. You will learn a lot from her. See you around Dar."

"Thank you, see you around."

Class went fairly quickly. Dar knew that he would excel at this course without a problem. As he exited class, he noticed the silver haired boy coming out of the classroom across from his. He was talking with two other boys: a chubby boy with red hair and a thin boy with honey colored hair that reminded him of a lion-fox's mane.

He turned his attention away from the boys and made his way to the cafeteria which, in his opinion, was the easiest place to find. All he did was follow his nose and the growling stomachs of his classmates.

Entering into the cafeteria he noted the one thing he hated the most about going to a new school - finding a seat. He concluded that it would be easier to get his meal first and then locate an open spot later. His decision panned out, finding a spot at the end of a table next to a purple-headed girl that he had seen in passing during the entrance exams. As he made his way across the cafeteria he hoped upon hope that no one would take that seat before he reached it. Immediately after he took the seat the girl next to the empty spot asked him to move.

"My sister is sitting there, but no one is sitting here." She pointed her smooth milk colored hand to a spot in front of her that just opened up. Dar shifted his position with an apology.

"It is no problem," she announced as she introduced herself as Aphreneea Anakin of the Anakin clan.

"Is this your first year at Helios?" she asked.

"Yes it is."

"Me too. My sister is Siren, Ren for short; it is our first year too. Gotten lost much?"

"Yes I did, but this third year student helped me out."

"Which one? Is he or she here?"

"Um….he is over there. The boy with the silver hair."

"Ohhh….nobody has helped us out. You are lucky."

"I guess."

"Oh….this is Siren," she said as a medium-sized green haired girl, the same complexion as her took a seat. "This is Dar, Siren."

"It is a pleasure to meet you. It is nice to finally talk to someone. This school can be a bit intimidating, however, not as much as those exams."

"They were a bit tough, but manageable," Aphreneea said confidently.

"Did you think your first test was hard? Ren questioned

"A little," he said with a shrug of his shoulders, "But it was manageable," he said with a smile as he let the conversation trail-off until the bell rang.

"Do you want to sit together tomorrow?" Siren asked.

Dar nodded his head and walked off to his fourth period class with the added security that he would not be sitting by himself tomorrow. His thoughts were quickly interrupted by the presence of the three older boys walking towards him.

"Thank you again for helping me find my second period class."

"It is no problem. I noticed when I looked on your schedule that my class was right across from yours during that period."

Looking at his friends, he cleared his throat and introduced them. He called the chubby one, Altis and the golden haired boy, Leo.

"I notice we have the same lunch period. Do you want to sit together tomorrow?"

"No thank you."

"Why not?" the golden haired boy said, with a little edge in his voice which caused Eres to jab him lightly in the side.

"What Leo meant to say is we understand. See you tomorrow Dar, during first period."

"Bye," Dar said as he turned to walk to his class.

When he turned the corner he paused for a second after hearing one of the boys say his name. After that, all he could make out was Leo saying over and over again, "Him."

When the bell rang, he had to leave, hearing the conversation trail off. He found his last class fairly quickly. The teacher excused his tardiness due to it being the first week of school.

This class was very boring—all they learned was how the borders developed between the regions. Looking around the class he noticed that he was the only one awake and there were still forty minutes left. He watched the clock tower's hands slowly move, minute to minute.

Gradually he began to fade out the teacher's voice and focused on the words he heard from Leo, "Him." What did he mean by him? Was he talking about me or someone else? His thoughts were broken when the bell sounded freedom.

Hastily, he broke through the pack of students to return to his dorm room. When he reached his room he fell across his bed, only to get back up when he heard a knock at his door. When he opened it there was no one around. He looked to the left and to the right, but there was no one.

"Games already," he sighed as he closed the door.

"No games at all," a voice said behind him.

Startled, he turned around, but no one was there. "Who's there?" he gasped. No one answered.

He swiftly left his room and walked towards the dormitory exit, which was quickly being blocked by stones rising from the floor and the walls.

"Who is doing this?" he yelled down the hall, only getting a reply from his echo.

He did not know whether to return to his room or to try to break the newly-formed wall down. Staying frozen in place he contemplated his move when a hard wind hit him from behind knocking him to the floor. Standing quickly to his feet, he scrambled back up and made a dash to his room, deciding that the window was his best escape. When he opened his door another gust of wind came and knocked him out of the room into the door across the hall.

"Enough!" he yelled. He got up, taking a firm stance and swung his arms in big circle creating a ring of fire with each pass of his arms. He then shot the swirling stream of fire at the stone entrance, but it was doused by rain.

"That will not stop me from getting out!" he announced, causing stones to form around his body like armor. He charged at the wall. As he was running, the ground under his feet became quicksand.

Dar pulled himself up from the sinking pit by turning his armor into a stone ladder attached to the ceiling. Out of breath, he stayed on the ladder waiting for the next thing to come. But as quickly as it formed, the wall blocking the entrance came crumbling down and the floor became solid again. When the wall fell he saw some of his classmates walking towards him from a distance. He jumped down from the ladder that became dust in the wind, and walked to the entrance when he was sure the floor would not change.

"Did you guys see that wall just now?" he asked when they arrived.

"No, we did not. How did you get back here so fast?" a boy asked him.

"I just walked here."

"I saw you walking, and then you were gone when I turned back around. You must have run."

"But I didn't," he declared.

"Alright, all I am saying is that you got here fast," the boy concluded as he walked past Dar into the dormitory building.

"But I didn't!" Dar said to himself as he looked back into the dormitory.

The following day, he went to his classes as though nothing had ever happened. However, he couldn't get his mind off of yesterday's events. His brain could not wrap itself around why those things happened. His thoughts were only interrupted when Aphreneea asked him a question.

"I am sorry, what did you say?"

"Did you hear anything that I was just saying to you Dar?" Aphreneea asked.

"I did not," he apologized.

But before she could restart her story Eres and his crew came by, causing several students to immediately get up and move away from the table.

"How about that, three open seats," Leo said as he sat down and looked towards Aphreneea who rolled her eyes at him and turned her back.

"Well, we thought if you could not sit with us today, that we will sit with you today," Eres announced as he took his seat next to Dar.

"Well, aren't you friendly," Aphreneea announced sarcastically.

"And you are?" Eres turned to look at the intrusive green eyed girl.

"I am Aphreneea, and you are?"

"Eres" he announced, which caused several other students to leave the table.

These actions did not go unnoticed by Aphreneea, who held her position on the other side of Dar.

"And what are your names?" she said pointing to the other two boys.

"How about your boyfriend?" Leo said leaning towards her.

"How about in your dreams?" she rebutted swiftly.

"Feisty, isn't she," Leo said to Eres.

"Very much so," he said looking over at her.

Wanting to break up the banter Dar said, "How can I help you guys?"

"We wanted to know if you wanted to hang out with us this afternoon?"

"Su….," but Aphreneea bumped his knee before he completed his sentence.

"Don't you remember that you said you would help me and Ren carry some things to the room? …you promised," she said, gently tapping his knee.

"I… Forgot," he said slowly and looked towards Eres, "I forgot."

"No problem. Catch you another time," he said as he left.

"What was that about?"

"You are very oblivious, aren't you?" she said as she pointed to the students who moved away from the table.

"They were done eating?" he was saying when she pointed to the very same students standing against the wall eating their food.

As the bell rang, the students filed out of the lunch room toward their fourth period class. The halls were crowded with students as Dar made his way to his locker to pick up his textbook. When he turned the corner toward the bank of lockers, he suddenly found himself outside in the woods. He looked around him as though he was in a dream.

"This is an illusion," he gasped.

"No illusion," a voice called out from the shadows.

"Who is there?"

"I don't like to be denied," the voice said again.

"What were you denied?"

"Your company," the voice said.

"Who are you?" Dar questioned before Eres, Altis, and Leo stepped from out a Traveler's rip.

"I tried the nice guy thing. I really did, but that is just not me," Eres said.

"I told you you would crack soon," Leo said putting his hand on his shoulder.

"I'm surprised you kept it up this long," Altis said.

"I did have some fun the other day though," Eres said looking back at his friends.

"What? It was you three," he spat at them.

"Well, it was mostly them two," Leo said pointing at his friends and laughing.

"Why?"

"You are quite an interesting person, Dar. Who would have guessed that a first year could be as developed as you are in their gifts? That whirl of fire was very impressive," Eres said as he stood in front of him, "But what else should I expect of a student of Helios."

"Let me pass," Dar demanded.

"Where are you going to go? You don't even know where you are? Let me tell you something, Dar Augustus. We rule this school. We can make you disappear just like that. How do you think you got to your dormitory so quickly the other day?" he said before adding, "Or even in the desert during your candidacy.

"What?! Wait! That was you all?" Dar said in shock and horror.

Laughing, Leo said again, "Mostly them two."

"If we were able to take you when you were surrounded by teachers, think about what we could do when they aren't looking," Eres said intensely.

"Why me? Why did you choose me?

"You look like an interesting person," Leo interrupted with more laugher.

"So do some of the others. What do you want from me?"

"We want to see what you are capable of," Eres said.

"And how will you do that?"

"By making you do a test."

"Test?"

"Let's use a different word other than test. How about dare? That sounds much friendlier."

"So if I do these dares, and pass, you will leave me alone."

"In a way."

"And if I don't do these dares you will make my life hard while I am here?"

"Or any other place you go, not just here."

"And if I tell the principal, I am doomed?"

"You catch on quickly Dar."

"I don't understand why you chose me," Dar said as he felt entrapment and isolation begin to creep in.

"You have caught our attention," Eres said placing a hand on his shoulder.

Shaking himself from the memory, Dar got up and left the room mumbling, "Those three."

He wandered around campus for several hours until he found himself standing in front Cona La'Sia's home. The little cottage seemed to be changing colors with the setting sun. He stared up at the little cottage until his attention was drawn away seeing Grace and Cona La'Sia coming from a distance. He waited outside of their house in the shadows as they arrived.

The reason that he was there eluded him, so he could not give them a reason why he was outside. He wanted Grace to hate him, he wanted her to go away from him, he wanted this strange girl out of his life. So why did he find himself outside of her home?

He focused his eyes on the little cottage when they entered the home. He watched as each room in the home became lit by a candle. Each flickering candle gradually caused the inhabitants' shadows to dance around the room, creating the illusion of more than two people. The once darkened house was now alive with life and motion.

He followed as one figure moved slowly from one floor to the other until it reached a small room facing the garden behind him. A small pale hand reached out of the window and pulled it closed. He examined the silhouette for a moment before recognizing it as Grace's.

'What am I doing?' he thought to himself as the words of his professor seeped to the surface of his memory. "Saving someone is not hurting that person you are trying to save." He sighed as the truth of those words became a hot dagger in his heart as he picked up a handful of small stones. Hesitantly, he threw the first stone.

When she opened the window she saw a spherical light and felt a smashing pain on her forehead. She grabbed her head and said, "What do you want Dar? You hurt me with your actions and now with a stone."

"Please come outside I want to tell you something," Dar said in a loud whisper.

"No, I will not. Go away Dar," said Grace as she shut the window and walked away.

However, when she turned around to the window she saw a bright light hovering at her window. Letting out a small scream as she stumbled backwards, she flipped over her bed to the other side. Peeking over the edge of the bed she heard a couple of raps at her window.

She slowly went over to the window and opened it and he said, "If you won't come down to me, I will come up to you."

"How did you get up here?" Grace said in a stunned voice.

"Remember Grace, I control the elements. I just raised the earth below my feet."

In a defeated voice Grace sat down on her bed and said, "What do you want Dar?" He sat down on the window ledge and said, "Well tonight is a beautiful night. The moon is shining and there is a cool breeze in the air."

"Well I don't know what the moon looks like and I will say again, what do you want Dar?"

"I have come to apologize."

"A sorry does not always make things better Dar. Remember, you don't want to have to babysit a poor blind girl, right?"

He took a deep breath. "I know an apology won't heal all the wounds I gave you today, but an apology with an explanation might. Please hear me out. I treated you so badly today because I don't want you to get hurt."

"Who would want to hurt me? I just got here."

"It is not you who they are trying to hurt, but me. You remember those boys and the dare?" Grace nodded. "I did not have a choice in doing it. It was not that I thought it was safe. I knew it was dangerous. But if I did not do it, I would not be here today. Those three boys, especially Eres, are to be feared. The only ones who could take them on are a few teachers, just a few. And they came to me the other day with another dare, a very dangerous dare. More so than the Varcus dare. They want me to get three feathers from the tail of the Phoenix on Fire Mountain. I agreed. But then they started to ask questions about you. Your name, if we were friends, and so on. And then Eres used his ability to make you fall. He is an Elementer also. He threatened in not so many words to bring you in on the dares. And I cannot allow that."

"What gives you the right to make that choice?" Grace challenged him after a moment of silence.

"No one."

"Yes no one, but I do understand and yes I do forgive. But I am not going to be chased off by anyone."

"I am not asking you to run, but I am asking you to please request that Aphreneea and Ren go around with you during the day. It is much safer, I'll make the arrangements."

"I am not afraid."

"You should be. Just ask."

"I don't know them Dar."

"Do you want to know death?"

"Sometimes I do."

"You are a stupid girl. If you do not ask I will make life with me so hard and unbearable for you. What you got today will be nothing to what I would put you through until you stay away from me."

"Is the problem with those boys that severe?"

"You have no idea. I've become a pawn in a game I don't understand and I don't want you to have to be a part of it."

"Fine. I will ask tomorrow."

"Thank you Grace," he said as he motioned to leave.

"Wait Dar, may I ask a request of you?" He nodded his head and said yes. "May I touch your face? I heard how you look, but I get a better picture when I touch something."

He picked up her hands and laid them against his face, his body moving before his mind thought. She ran her hands through his hair and said, "it is short" with a slight giggle. She then ran her hands across his lips, over his eyes, and down the bridge of his nose. Her hands glided over his cheek bones and down his ears. She said to him, "You do have a very beautiful face just like I heard."

Then suddenly there was a knock at the door and La'Sia walked in with a candle in her hand. She looked at Grace who was standing up at the window and said sleepily, "Grace is everything okay in here? I heard voices."

"Everything is just fine, just fine," she said with a smile as she turned to the window and saw Dar's light moving quickly away from the house toward the school. "Everything is just fine," she repeated.

With a slight yawn La'Sia said, "Okay…deary….Good night."

Chapter Six

Hello Girls

Bobbing down the steps with an extra spunk in her step, Grace coached herself on what she was going to say to the principal when she arrived at school. She had the perfect plan that would get Dar out of his obligation while allowing him to save face.

When La'Sia saw her smiling face come around the corner she said, "Did you have a good night sleep?"

"I did, and yourself?"

"Fairly peaceful. Are you ready to go?" La'Sia asked.

"I am ma'am."

When they arrived at school Dar was nowhere to be found. Crossing her arms, Grace felt her plan slipping away as she listened to La'Sia question Dar's whereabouts.

"I don't know," said the principal as she came out of her office, "I am going to…" but before she could finish her sentence

Aphreneea and Ren came into the office calling the principal's name.

"Yes. What can I do for you ladies?"

"We came to get Grace for the day," they said at the same time.

"Why?" she asked.

"Because Dar is sick," Aphreneea lied.

"Ohh…he seemed well yesterday," said the principal curiously.

"You know how these things go cona," Siren said.

"Well, Grace let's be off," said Aphreneea in effort to leave before the adults fully process the situation, "Ren and I don't want to be late for our first period class."

"Do you girls have the same classes this year?" asked La'Sia.

"We do," the sisters answered in sequence as they waved good-bye.

"Good bye, Cona La'Sia and Principal Zarena," Grace said as she felt the hand of one of the girls pulling her towards the door.

When they left the office Grace faced one of the girls and said, "Where is Dar?"

"I don't know. A note was under my door this morning and it said to pick you up in the office and tell Cona La'Sia that he was sick," Aphreneea said.

"Why would you do it for him?" Grace questioned.

"Because it also read that he would take me to the dance if I looked after you for a few days," she said.

"Ohhh…how noble you are," Grace grunted under her breath. "What do you get out of this exchange, Siren?"

"Nothing," she said simply.

"Then why do it?"

"No reason in particular. I have all the same classes as my sister so why not help her? Plus I already have my date for the dance. But enough about me," Siren said when they entered their first period class, "We are going to be together for a few days. Tell us a little about you so that it won't be so awkward between us," said Siren.

"What do you want to know?"

"Everything," Aphreneea said, taking the seat next to her.

"Well, my name is Grace Comings and I am from Stone Falls," she began.

"We already know that. Do you have a boyfriend back home?"

"My goodness. I do not."

"Why do you answer like that, like it is a strange question?" asked Aphreneea.

"Because…because…because."

"Because what?" said Siren.

"Because…" but before she could answer the teacher began class.

"Don't think this conversation is over with," said Aphreneea, smiling at Grace.

Aphreneea and Ren's first period teacher was different from Dar's, and the first woman teacher she heard since being in the building. She was a well-educated woman from what Grace could decipher. She taught on the cosmos. She explained the rotation of the sun and the moon, talked about distant galaxies as though she had been there herself. Grace never thought about other places outside of the Earth.

She soon found herself asking the teacher questions and getting answers she never thought imaginable.

"So there are other planets out there?" Grace said.

"Of course, but they cannot be lived on," the professor answered.

"Why not?"

"Because the planets in our galaxies are not made for us. There may not be enough air, or it may be too hot or too cold, or there may not even be ground to stand on."

"I did not know," Grace said out loud as the bell rang.

Packing up her bag Siren said, "Wow Grace you asked questions like you have never been in school before."

"I have never been to school before. This is my first time," she said.

"They don't have a school in Stone Falls?" asked Aphreneea.

"Of course they do, but when my mother died my aunt would not allow me to go," Grace said, thinking that that was close enough to the truth.

"Your mother died?" Siren said.

"Yes. Two years ago."

"I am so sorry to hear that," said Aphreneea.

"Why did your aunt not allow you to go to school?" Siren said.

"Because I am a poor ugly blind girl who does not need an education," replied Grace as though she had rehearsed the words of her aunt over and over again.

"Your aunt sounds horrible," Siren said.

"You have no idea," Grace mumbled.

Aphreneea noted that the conversation had taken a turn for the worse, so she started up a new conversation as they entered into their second period.

"Well, let us tell you about us now," she said noticing they arrived a bit early. "My name is Aphreneea Anakin and this is my sister Siren Anakin. Our clan, the Anakin clan, are known for being Myth Seers and great merchants."

"Who do you sell to?"

"We sell to everyone all over Geo," Aphreneea answered, "I personally have been to all the great Lands, with the exception of one, the Ice Lands. It's too cold and Father does very little busy on that Land."

"I've only been to five of the great Lands," Ren sorrowfully interjected.

"What do you sell?"

"Clothing, spice, medicine, jewelry, food, games, almost anything," Aphreneea said.

"Then your family must be very wealthy."

"We do well for ourselves," Aphreneea said as she flung her hair gently over her shoulder.

"Is it hard to sell across the borders," Grace said puzzlingly.

"Not really, my father, his brothers, and his sisters have been in this profession for generations. It is to the point that borders almost are non-existent to my family. Besides, we are so spread about all of Geo, that I have relatives living on all the great Lands. However, our father is the head of all the families," Aphreneea concluded.

"So you are like princesses," Grace said.

"I would not go that far," Aphreneea said.

"Do you have other siblings?"

"We do, an older brother, named Sadee"

"But he becomes sick too often and cannot really help Father on his travels," Ren said.

"Therefore, my sister and I are in line to becoming the heads of the Northern Lands in the years to come," she said looking over at her sister, "But Ren doesn't want to."

"You can have it, sister. I am not interested in walking in Father's shoes."

"I still don't understand why," her sister said shaking her head.

"What do you want to do then?" Grace questioned.

"To become an artist," Aphreneea answered for her.

"Yes, I want to be an artist."

"What type of art do you want to make?" Grace questioned.

"Paintings," she said happily, "Because of our Father's profession we see a lot of things. And I want to paint those things and bring a piece of Geo into every Geoians home. I want to paint things from the Northern Lands to the Desert Lands to the Ice

Lands, from all of Geo," she said as she waved her arms in an arch pattern.

"We sell art," was all Aphreneea could say.

"It's not the same."

"You mentioned earlier that you were Myth Seers? What is a Myth Seer?"

"We can make anyone see anything we want them to see," said Siren. "We can make them see a lie, an illusion."

"We can place them in a beautiful garden, or have them falling off a cliff," Aphreneea said.

"That sounds like an amazing gift," said Grace.

"It comes in handy," said Aphreneea looking at a boy across the room, who quickly looked down, "That is why the merchant trade is a great path for people with our gifts. The more exposure we have to different things, the more creative our illusions can be."

"Do you have to see something to be able to use it in an illusion?'

"No, not really," Aphreneea said thinking about it for a moment, "But I have personally discovered that the more you are exposed to something the quicker you can use it in an illusion and the more creative you can be," she concluded when the bell rang for the class to begin.

During a group activity, Eres came up to Siren after he saw Aphreneea walk away. "I noticed that you were talking to Dar's friend over there," he said looking at Grace standing across the room, "Do you know a lot about her?" Eres asked.

"I-I don't know her too well," she said, a little smitten and frightened that he was even talking to her.

"Tell me a little about what you do know about her," Eres said as he gently removed a stray hair from her cheek.

"Well she is from…" but before she could have a chance to explain Aphreneea came over.

"What do you want Eres?" asked Aphreneea callously.

"I just wanted to know about your new friend. That is all," removing his hand from her sister's cheek.

"Well her name is Grace and that is all you need to know."

"Aphreneea, who do you think you are speaking to?" he said, smooth but strong.

"What are you going to do about it Eres?" she said calmly as she stepped slightly towards him, "Maybe you have everyone one else in this school afraid to breathe around you, but I am not one of them."

"You should be," he said as he walked away.

"What are you doing Siren?" Aphreneea chastened her sister.

"He just wanted to know a little about Grace," she said.

"If he wants to know anything it must be that he is up to no good."

"You are so brave around him," her sister said.

"Because I refuse to allow him to make me afraid," she said. "Where is Grace?"

Her sister pointed to the window Grace was looking out of. When she walked over she said, "What are you doing?"

"Just thinking."

"About?"

"Nothing really."

"Well the teacher is beckoning us to sit down," said Aphreneea. "The class is almost over, just ten minutes left."

As they took their seats the teacher gave them last minute instructions on the project that was due in three days. After the bell rang, Aphreneea purposely told Siren and Grace to wait because she wanted Eres to leave the room first.

When she was sure he was gone she left with the two girls. "Siren, I left my fourth period book in my locker and it is on the other side of the school. Can you take Grace to the lunch room?"

"You can use mine sister."

"And have professor Lynos give me another speech on responsibility? I don't think so," she said. "I will be there in ten minutes," she continued, waving her hands for them to go.
When she was sure that they were gone she ventured to the north side of the school to retrieve her book. Upon approaching her locker she saw three boys standing by it.

"Well, well fancy meeting you here, Aphreneea," said Eres.

"Being that this is my locker – I don't see the fancy."

"That mouth of yours has gotten you in trouble," he said.

"And you had to bring your boys with you to deal with little old me," she said crossing her arms to hide the fact that they started to shake.

"You are bold," he said as he started to walk towards her. "What? You are not going to run away?"

"Why should I run? I came to get something and I will get it." She truly wanted to run but fear anchored her feet to the floor.

He then rushed at her, and she promptly created an illusion around her in defense.

"Nice job, Aphreneea" he said, finding himself in the middle of a jungle. "I think the animals are a little much."

"Why do you want to know so much about Grace?" She watched the three boys, able to see both the deception and the reality as though they were one. It was as though there were two pictures laid on top of one another.

"That is none of your concern," he said as he looked around at the hanging vines and the fruit-laden trees. "You know I will find you eventually," he announced as he strategically grabbed at empty space.

"All I have to do is wait out the bell."

"I notice you have not moved much."

"I am not stupid. You are not going to gizba me. I understand that some of you Elementers can feel out movement through the ground and being that this is a small area, I am not going to move. I do know something about Elementer's abilities."

Eres moved slightly towards her voice and reached his arm out when he found himself in the Ice Lands. "Did I get too close to you?" he said cockily.

Silence was her only reply as she looked around for a means of escape. He was getting closer to her and she could only shift her position slightly between each illusion. If she moved too much her position would be revealed.

"So, no more words from you… Leo and Altis, don't move," he said as he started to shoot off tiny rocks in every direction.

"What are you doing?" Altis asked.

"Getting my bearings. There we go," he announced as he raised up two stone walls causing the only exits to be blocked. "Now that should do it."

Aphreneea looked up at the two massive stone walls and saw that there was no escape. The blood in her veins began to race and her muscles began to tighten.

"I felt it. Panicked are we? Now it is just the four of us," Eres announced.

"How long do you think you can keep those walls up before someone comes along and sees them?" she said breaking her silence.

"I will find you momentarily, Aphreneea. You are gifted but you made one mistake," he said as he reached out quickly and caught her by the throat.

"You moved." The illusion dissolved around them and his stone walls dropped. He slammed her against the locker and she heard the other boys laughing in the background.

Through the choking grip she mustered, "Only. One. Step."

"That was enough. Your illusions can not work if I feel the one who is emitting it," he said touching her cheek slowly with his pointer finger.

"Now tell me Aphreneea, everything you know about this Grace girl, and I will let you go."

"I don't know anything," she said as her feet began to hover above the ground.

He slammed her back into the lockers and yelled, "Liar!"

"Save yourself some pain and tell him what he needs to know," Leo spoke out through laugher.

She struggled to look over at Leo, but when she made eye contact she said, "Shut. Up."

Eres tightened his grip on her neck and looked at her strangely. His icy eyes looked into hers, reading a story he could only see. Suddenly, Aphreneea became afraid of what he was thinking. Then he let her go.

He stood over her for a few minutes watching the purple-headed girl take in several deep breaths. He bent down to her and whispered slowly into her ear, "I see it now."

With her eyes still focused on the stone floor, she took a shallow breath and said fragilely, "What do you see?"

"Fear," he said slowly as he stood back up and walked towards the boys. Leo spoke out and said, "What about the information on the Grace girl?"

"That can come later. I captured something worth a little more than that."

Aphreneea continued to stare at the ground until she was sure they had walked away. Then she got up slowly, retrieved her book from the locker, and walked to the cafeteria where Eres and his crew were waiting at the entrance with a few professors.

"Hi Aphreneea," said Eres in a kind voice as she passed by him.

"Are you not going to answer, Aphreneea?" one of the professors said.

"I am sorry cono. I did not hear him," she lied looking into his smug eyes. "What did you say Eres?"

"I said 'Hello,'" he repeated.

"Hello Eres. How are you?"

"I am well. Thank you for asking. Tell me, who is that young lady with your sister?"

She paused and saw that she was trapped. The professor said, "Yes, who is she?"

"Her name is Grace, cono," Aphreneea answered.

"That is a strange name. Where is she from?" quickly asked Eres.

"Yes. That is a strange name. Where is she from?" asked the professor, looking at Aphreneea.

"She is from Stone Falls, cono," looking at Eres smiling at her from behind the two professors.

The second professor asked if she was kin to her and her sister. "That is a good question. For I believe all Anakin's have green hair or eyes, or purple hair or eyes," said Eres.

"Yes that is true, very true," the second professor said.

"She is no kin to our family," she answered shortly.

"And yet you have been taking her around all day," Eres said.

"Yes, why?" asked the first professor.

Aphreneea sighed and said, "Because Dar asked us to, cono. For he was sick today."

At that, Eres smiled evilly and said, "So she is kin to Dar."

"I thought Dar did not have any kin," the first professor said to the second.

"She is a friend of Dar, cono" replied Aphreneea.

"A friend," Eres said. "I thought he said she was not his friend."

"I have to go. Please excuse me," said Aphreneea.

The second professor called out to her and said, "Tell that young girl to tell Dar I hope he feels better."

"I will cono," Aphreneea said as she walked to the table and sat down.

"You were gone for a long time," Siren said.

"Problems," she said looking towards Eres and back to Grace, "What are you in to?"

"I don't understand," Grace said.

"Why is Eres and his crew after you?" she whispered intensely.

"They are?" Grace played stupid.

"Yes they are," Aphreneea said a little baffled.

"Is that a bad thing?"

"A bad thing? Yes Grace that is a bad thing," she said wiping her purple hair out of her face. "You have no idea."

"Did they hurt you, sister?"

"I am a little shaken, but I am okay."

"Let's go tell the principal," Siren suggested.

"What good is that going to do? What happened to the last person who told on them?"

"I don't know. She just left the school one day to attend another school," she said thinking back on her classmate.

"Yeah. Leave this school or else," said Aphreneea.

Interjecting into the conversation, Grace said, "Can you tell me a little about them, this Eres and his crew?"

"What can we say about them?" Ren said looking at her sister, "Except that they are absolutely the best in their representative gifts," she said with a hint of admiration.

"Nevertheless," Aphreneea asserted, "I think this leads them to a sense of superiority and self-entitlement."

"Why do you think that?"

"It is in their treatment of others," she said as she rubbed her neck, "They think they can treat people anyway they please, because they are so strong."

"Is everyone afraid of them?"

"Most and even some teachers," said Ren

"That is why it is sometimes pointless telling on them," Aphreneea added

"Is everyone in their families as strong as they are?" Grace questioned

"Who knows?" Aphreneea shrugged her shoulders, "They won't let anyone get close enough to them to find out."

"Ummm….that depends on which one you're talking about, sister" Ren said as she thought through the laundry list of girls that Leo has gone through.

"That is a different type of close," Aphreneea corrected her.

"If I understand correctly, Eres is the leader, right?" Grace asked

"Yes, he is," said Aphreneea.

"How many are there in his group, again?"

"Three," Ren said, "Eres, the Elementer, Altis, the Traveler, and Leo, the Shapeshifter,"

"Then who follows Eres in the chain of command, Altis or Leo?"

"I don't know who would be the second in command of the trio, but it always appears that Altis is more obedient than Leo. Both of them listen without question to Eres, but it sometimes appears that Leo is more reckless with his actions."

"I see. So, Eres is probably the one who formed this group."

"Most likely."

"So, if there isn't an Eres, then there isn't a group."

"I wouldn't go that far. Leo and Altis are extremely strong, they can survive without Eres, but their loyalty lies with Eres."

"Why?"

"Eres is a great leader," Ren said

"However, he is the type of leader to cause wars, instead of end them," Aphreneea was saying when the lunch bell rang to signal its end.

"Should we go and see Dar then?" said Grace.

"I think that is best," Aphreneea said.

"But he is sick," said Siren.

"Come on sister, do you really believe Dar, the overachiever, would miss school?" said Aphreneea. "We can skip our fourth period and go visit him."

"Would that not give a clue to Eres and his crew that Dar is not really sick?" said Grace.

"Maybe. But I do not want to stay in this school any longer today," Aphreneea said.

"Why don't you take Grace to see Dar and I can go to class? I can make up a reason why you are not there," Siren said.

"Good idea, sister," she said as she stood.

"We will make pretend we are going to class and then I will leave with Grace," Aphreneea said, walking towards the door. "Pretend to laugh," she said before breaking into a boisterous laugher as she passed by Leo and Altis at the door.

When they were sure that the boys were not following them, Siren went to class while Grace and Aphreneea went to Dar's dormitory as planned. When they arrived they knocked on his door but no one answered. "I know he is here. Dar is not a runner."

"Dar, open up, it is Aphreneea," she yelled while banging on the door. His next door neighbor suddenly came out a little irritated and said that Dar was out back practicing.

When they walked around back Grace could see Dar's light and heard a gasp from Aphreneea. "What is it?"

"It's Dar," she said a little girly.

"And?" Grace said annoyed.

"It's Dar with no shirt on," she added on to her original sentence.

"It is not polite to see a gentleman with his shirt off," Grace said to her as she called out Dar's name.

"What are you doing here?" he said when he came over.

"I should say the same thing," Aphreneea said, "Sick, huh."

She then paused and said, "I don't know what you tried to pull leaving Grace with us, but it did not work. You nearly got me hurt today, my mouth did not help the situation either, but…" she stopped.

"What! What happened?!" Dar said looking at Aphreneea up and down.

"Eres wanted to know about Grace," she said.

"Did you tell him anything?" he said looking at Grace.

"At first I did not tell him anything when he trapped me down by the lockers."

"Trapped you?"

"That is nothing. My mouth made him angrier than me not telling him about Grace. But when I came down to the cafeteria he was near some teachers and he used them like puppets to get the information he wanted."

"So he knows."

"He knows that this girl means more to you than us."

"I am sorry that I put you in harm's way, but thank you for your help."

"You're welcome, and no problem," she said brushing off his comment, "Will I see you at the gala on the night of the seventh moon?"

"A promise is a promise," he said.

Pausing from walking away, she turned and said, "Don't worry about it. I will catch you at the next gala. It does not feel right to go to the gala under these pretenses."

When Aphreneea left, Grace turned to him saying, "I guess your plan did not work."

"I guess not."

"What should we do now?"

"I don't know any more Grace. I just don't know. Let's go inside," he said guiding her to his dorm hall. However, their destination was blocked when Dar looked up to see Altis waiting in the doorway of the dormitory.

"Wow. You are feeling better Dar. I was sent over here to see if you needed anything. But I see that you got your medicine," he said looking at Grace.

"You came to spy on me Altis," he clarified.

"You found me out," he said clapping his hands, "I am sure that Eres will be pleased with my report. Did you think your act the other day fooled us Dar?"

"It was not an act."

"Sure Dar. But anyway I am off, back to campus. I will see you tomorrow," he said as he created a rip and jumped through it.

Dar sighed deeply and said nothing as he guided Grace to his room. "Here, take a seat," he said walking toward his clothing trunk to find a clean shirt.

"What's the new plan?" Grace asked.

"To keep you safe until we are able to get you back home."

"So you are not going to leave me with a stranger again?"

"There's no point to it now." He took a seat next to her on the bed.

"I think you will be in trouble tomorrow with Principal Zarena."

"That is okay," he said as he lay back on his bed. He looked over to Grace who was facing the window.

"What are you thinking about?"

"Nothing really. Just home."

"You really want to get back don't you?"

"In a way, yes, because it is familiar. I can go around and know where I am going. I don't need my sight back home. But this place is so unfamiliar. I never truly felt blind until I came to this place. I feel helpless and burdensome."

Saying nothing he looked up at his ceiling as he felt Grace lean back against his arm.

He looked at her icy eyes pointed up at the ceiling, and found himself drifting off to sleep. He did not realize that he was asleep until the bell sounded signaling that fourth period was over.

He sat up quickly, looking around, when he saw Grace once again staring out the window.

"I am sorry I fell asleep."

"You were tired. There is nothing to be sorry about that."

"Are you ready to go?"

"Yes I am."

When they arrived at La'Sia's home she was surprised that he was feeling better and was kind enough to bring Grace back home.

"Will we see you tomorrow?" she asked him.

"I believe so."

Chapter Seven

Fire Mountain

The following morning Grace awoke early to the sound of birds singing outside of her window. The sun had barely broken the surface of the midnight sky when she heard a tap against her window. Jerking up she looked toward the window when she heard another tap. She climbed slowly out of bed and walked cautiously over the cold wooden floor to the window. When she reached the open window the cool morning breeze filled her senses as the wind gently blew her hair away from her face. Grace leaned her body out of the window and whispered, "Hello!?...is anyone there? ... Dar is that you? I can't see you."

Suddenly Grace heard a hard, ominous voice said, "No, it is not," as she was pulled out of her room. Grace did not have the chance to scream, the shock of the intruder paralyzed her with fear. Grace felt herself moving swiftly across the yard held under the arm of the intruder who smelled strongly of lavender.

When she was finally able to speak, she demanded his name and where he was taking her.

"Hush!" the intruder said viciously.

Grace stubbornly continued, "Who are you?"

The intruder stopped, tightened his hands around her neck, and slowly said, "If you speak again I will kill you here and leave your body to rot. Your life means very little to me, but I have my orders, but mistakes happen."

She wanted to know where the intruder's orders came from, but she dared not to speak again.

'I refuse to cry…I refuse to cry…I will not cry…' Grace wiped a single tear from her eye as she was lifted back up by the intruder.

'Dar…Cona La'Sia…Principal Zarena…where are you?'

La'Sia still cloaked in her blankets let out a drowsy yawn as the sun started to peek its way through her window. Turning over in her bed as the sun rays crawled towards her, she let out a small grunt in an attempt to scare them away.

Peeking from out of her blankets she let out a small sigh as the clock chimed half past six. Shaking the tangled blankets from off of her, she climbed out of her bed and drowsily made her way to Grace's room. Knocking lightly on the door she called out Grace's name. Not hearing her normal response, she knocked again and received the same outcome. Gently pushing open the door she saw that the bedroom was empty.

Thinking that she may have gone outside without her seeing or hearing her, La'Sia walked to the backyard as she called out Grace's name. However, her response was still the same – silence. Running to the front yard she again yelled Grace's name – to no avail.

"Maybe she went with Dar already," she said as she quickly got dressed and wrapped a shawl around her shoulders.

When she reached the office she managed to say with the last vestige of her breath, "Dar, where is Grace?"

"I don't know. I was waiting here for you two to come in."

"Oh…my goodness," she said as she fell in a nearby chair.

Dar walked over to her as she raised her head. "Grace is gone."

"What? How? When? …it's impossible," Dar said, "Maybe she walked to school on her own?"

"She does not know her way yet."

"Good morning everyone," the principal said cheerfully when she walked into the office.

"It is not a good morning," replied Dar.

"Why is that so my dear boy?"

"Grace is missing."

"When did this happen?" the principal said, swiftly taking off her shawl.

"Last night I think, I don't know what time," replied La'Sia, "What are we going to do?"

"Send out a Siphona to the Trackers to see if they will give us assistance," replied the principal, "Their strong senses will give us some information on where she went."

"Shouldn't we check the school grounds?" asked Dar.

"The Trackers will do that when they get here," the principal said, "If Grace was taken then they will be able to find her position quicker than we could looking over this campus."

"I will go call them now," La'Sia said as she raced towards a Siphona.

"Dar, I need you to go to class and not to say a word of this to anyone."

"But Principal Zarena, I can help…don't make me go to class. If Grace is in trouble, I can help," he said pleading.

"Your ability is under developed, you cannot help us … please go to class," replied the principal.

"But…" Dar paused. "Yes cona," he said as he bitterly walked out of the office.

Reaching his first class, he sat down at his desk next to her empty chair and looked out of the window. Aphreneea and Ren noticed that something was off about Dar, so during their break they approached him.

"What is wrong Dar Augustus?" questioned Aphreneea.

Never making eye contact, he said, "Nothing is the matter."

"Don't lie to me Dar, something is the matter," said Aphreneea forcefully, "And where is Grace?"

At the mention of Grace's name, Dar turned quickly to face Aphreneea. She pulled back, knowing now that she had touched a sore topic, and said to Ren, "Come on let's go."
When Dar saw that they were gone, he turned back around placing his head in his hand as he looked out the window, 'Grace where are you?'

As the bell sounded, he hastily got out of his seat and raced to the office to get an update. When he arrived at the office the Trackers were there. Dar recognized them immediately from the pictures in his textbook. He recalled that Trackers are the Ivoro People of the North Mountain. However, he never imagined that he would see one, one day.

Inching his way towards the office door to get a closer look, he noticed that each one had a distinctive pattern of their own on their fur coat. However, their coats appeared very thin to the point that Dar thought it lay down like a person's skin. With the exception of their hair which was cut differently on each one of their heads. They could, in his opinion, be considered a close relative of the Varcus even though they appeared almost person-like. Nevertheless, his assessment came to an end when he heard one of them talking.

"We went to La'Sia's house and we followed the scent all the way to the campus walls. It smells as though this intruder has taken the Grace girl off of campus."

"Oh…my goodness, what are we to do?" said La'Sia, pacing back and forth.

"We can go after her…the scent is still fresh, but there is a problem," the lead Tracker said.

"What? What is the problem?" said the principal.

"The smell of the intruder is common to four places in the realm of Geo. We can track them, but only so far before we will have to split into teams," said the lead Tracker.

"What is that smell?" replied La'Sia.

"It is the smell of lavender. This plant grows near the four giant mountains: The Wind Mountain, The Water Mountain, The Earth Mountain, and The Fire Mountain," the Tracker replied.

'Fire Mountain, those fools…they wouldn't. Or would they?' Dar thought as he ran from the office toward the south wing of the school where he knew he would find Eres.

Running through the south wing corridor, he saw Eres in the distance. He ran up to him and threw him against the wall yelling, "What did you do with Grace?!"

In a calm, smooth voice he said, "I don't know what you are talking about. Did you lose something special?"

"Don't play with me Eres, What did you do with GRACE!!!"

"You poor foolish boy. Do you think your little show of hating that girl worked?"

"Eres," Dar grunted slowly.

"Who do you think you are talking to? You must have forgotten your place, second year, and who you are dealing with."

"I have not forgotten nothing."

"Then release me, boy. Before you get hurt."

"I will not!" said Dar slamming Eres against the wall again.

Smiling suddenly, Eres lifted his hands as a stone wall sprung up from the ground separating him and Dar. Dar soon found himself in mid-air being cut from every angle by razor sharp winds before he was thrown down the hallway. Some students in the hallway ran away from the attack, while others stopped to watch. When Dar hit the floor his head, arms, and legs were covered in blood.

"Who do you think you are second year?! I can squash you like the bug you are!"

"I am the one who is going to take you down," Dar said slowly as he got up and wiped the blood from his mouth. "I am the ONE!" he yelled, starting to charge at Eres.

Eres let out five fireballs from his hands which were destined for Dar's body when the hallways became dark and the sound of thunder ripped from forming clouds. Abruptly there came a downpour of rain. Dar ceased his charge as the fireballs were extinguished by the rain. Professor Lynos walked outside of his classroom and said, "There is to be no fighting within the walls of this school. You two know the rules. Go to class. Now! Dar come in here and sit down."

"That is fine with me," Eres said as he started to walk away. Shortly he stopped and looked over his shoulder and said, "Hey Dar, it is easy to dodge fire when you see it coming, but what happens when you can't?"

Grace shrieked when she touched another hot piece of stone. Rubbing her burnt hand on her floral night gown she screamed out for help.

"I would keep quiet girl. For if you wake up the Phoenix you are dead," the lavender-scented intruder said.

"The Phoenix? What is your name, sir?"

"That is none of your concern," replied the intruder as he started to walk out the cave entrance. "I think you should stay still, or face death…for you are surrounded by steam vents and pools of liquid fire."

"So how did you get me over here?"

Leaving out of the cave the intruder did not reply as he looked at the narrow walkway that separated her from the freedom she desired.

When the bell rang Dar started to race out of the classroom, but Professor Lynos called after him. "Here Dar, take this, I think it will be helpful to you one day," he said as he handed Dar a brown leather bound book.

"What is this cono?" Dar said.

Lynos simply replied, "Just a book."

Dar opened the book as he left the classroom and saw that it was a book of maps to the four great mountains. Dar turned around to his professor.

"Just a book that I thought you would like," he simply said.

"Thank you, cono," Dar said rubbing his hand along the cover of the book as he walked down the hallway. When he looked up he saw Altis and Leo blocking his path, "What do you want?" Dar said angrily.

"Just to remind you that today is the third day and the gala is on the night of the seventh moon and it is an awfully long walk to a certain mountain. I calculate that it will take at least two days…good-day old boy," Leo said.

Boiling with rage, Dar desired to attack the two boys as they walked away, but he knew that if he was injured anymore he could not help Grace. So, he looked at the floor and started to count backwards from one hundred. When he reached the number one he ran out of the school toward the drawbridge.

He knew he could not take the bridge exit, because it was forbidden for students to leave the campus during the school day without a letter of permission. Looking at the high walls he knew that someone would see him if he tried to go over, and there was no time to wait until dark.

He then opened the book professor Lynos gave him to determine if it truly was a two day journey to the Fire Mountain. When he opened the book and turned to the page that had the map of Fire Mountain on it, a little piece of paper fell out onto the ground.

Picking up the small piece of folded paper, he cautiously unfolded it to discover that it was a permission slip for him to leave the Campus early. He looked back at the window of his professor's room to see him standing framed in the window.

'Just a book, huh, professor,' Dar thought. When Dar saw the shadowy figure of his professor draw into the darkness of his classroom he turned around and rushed towards the drawbridge.

When he arrived he let out a huge yell, "Let down the draw-bridge!"

At this command a strong but elderly voice rang out from the walls of the drawbridge, "Who is this that gives me a command like he is my master?"

"It is I, Dar Augustus."

"Dar Augustus," the wall said, emphasizing every "s" in every word he spoke.

"Please let me pass, I have a pass," Dar said. Upon this statement a face formed in the wood of the drawbridge. "Let me see your pass young man."

When Dar lifted up the pass to the face of the wall all you could hear was, "Yes I see, ummmm...Professor Lynos....I know him good man...for Dar Augustus...okay...okay." Dar slowly pulled back the pass, "May I pass by Arbol?"

"Cono Arbol to you, boy," he said.

"I am sorry, may I pass Cono Arbol?"

"You may pass, but the next time you climb over my walls you are in trouble young man...I let you have some fun, but I did not appreciate that the principal told me that you went to the Whispering Woods."

"How did you know I climbed your wall? It was all the way on the other side."

"Young boy, do you think I am just the wood to this drawbridge? I am the wall and the wall is me."

At this statement Dar became infuriated. "Then why did you not stop someone from stealing Grace? …If you are the wall and the wall you…you could have done something…but you did nothing…nothing to help her."

"Calm down young lad…this person went by air. I have no control over the air. I just thought it was a couple of students going out together. But I am tired," Arbol said as he lowered the bridge for Dar.

Dar stomped across the whole bridge then looked back at the wall and said, "You did nothing," as it drew back up.

"Principal Zarena, have you seen Dar? I went to the cafeteria and he was not there," said La'Sia.

"No, I have not, but I have spoken to his first and second period teachers and they said that he was in class," replied the principal. "Do you think that he went off to search for Grace?"

"It is a possibility," replied La'Sia.

"You know he has no family, right, La'Sia?"

"No, I did not know that. What brought up that thought?

"I don't know, to tell you the truth. I have not thought about it in such a long time."

"What happened to his family?"

"It happened about eight years ago…long before he came to this school. I only know the story told to me by the principal of his previous school. Who himself heard it from someone Dar spoke to the day of the incident," said Zarena. "Let me see…the past principal said that Dar and his father went on a normal hunting trip when they came across this creature."

"A creature…what type of creature?"

"No one knows…but it managed to slaughter over thirty Travelers in the forest that day. Their bodies were badly torn and pieces were scattered all over the ground and the trees. The white flowers on the ground were stained red from their blood.

It was a massacre. They said that it looked like there were streams of blood running through the grass."

"Oh my goodness," La'Sia said, covering her mouth.

"However, one Traveler survived. He was badly wounded to the point of death when Dar's father came upon him. When his father saw him, he picked the Traveler up and placed Dar on his back. But the attacking creature was moving too fast and was about to catch up…so…."

"So…Dar's father left him – dropped the Traveler."

"Yes, it would be a choice that many parents would have made. He dropped the Traveler and ran as quickly as he could with Dar. While running, he could only put up earthen walls to slow down this creature, and it was of no use. It was too fast and too strong. Then, Dar's father decided to make a grave sacrifice…"

"His life…" said La'Sia.

"His life for the life of his son…he stopped running, put Dar down, and told him to run home as fast as he could. Dar's father battled with this creature with all of his might. When Dar arrived home he told his mother about his father and she ran out after her husband, telling Dar to stay there and they would be back.

"But they never came back…" replied La'Sia sadly.

"No they never came back…the creature tore them apart," said the principal.

"But I thought they were some of the most powerful Elementers there were," said La'Sia.

"Yes they were, but this creature….. The bodies of Dar's mother and father were so badly torn that they were not seen at the funeral. The last memory Dar has of his family is that of his father fighting, his mother's panic, and their coffins being engulfed in the fire. I was at that funeral…Dar tried to go into the fire to be with his parents, but he was held back. I can still remember his cries. Such cries should never be heard from a child."

"Then why is Dar the way he is today? I would think that he would hate the world, but I do not see that in him" asked La'Sia.

"That is a question that you will have to ask Dar. Well come on…the Trackers should be leaving in several hours.

The forest passed in a brown blur as Dar ran down a lightly worn dirt path. All the leaves had dropped to the ground leaving the trees standing noble and nude. The only sounds Dar could hear were the crunching of the foliage under his feet and the screaming thoughts in his head. Thoughts he would not dare to utter. Thoughts he would one day challenge himself to forget.

With each passing thought he pressed on faster and harder towards Grace, until unsuspectingly his body collapsed under him, causing him to tumble and flip viciously along the ground. When he finally came to a stop he tried to right his position only to fail with his legs rebelling against his commands to move. Looking at them, he tried to will them to budge to no avail.

In a last effort to stand, he began to drag his body towards a nearby tree hoping to use it for some leverage. However, he brought himself to an immediate stop when he felt excruciating pain shooting up and down his legs. As he paused for the first time, his thoughts were gradually replaced by the pounding of his heart threatening to escape from his chest. He lay facing the ground for a moment gasping for air - only to receive dirt and dry leaves.

His head began to ache and his vision began to blur. He suddenly noticed that the sun had set deeply into the western sky, indicating that he had been running hard for nearly six hours. With the last ounce of his strength he formed an earthen shelter and a small fire nearby. As he painfully pulled himself into the shelter, he laughed bitterly at his situation.

His only comfort came from knowing he was on the right path to save Grace. His attention was soon drawn away by an overwhelming need for water, but he had no strength left to draw it from the ground, so he turned his focus to the dancing flames that mocked his thirst.

The flames that so resembled those at his parents' funeral. "It is all my fault….I wished I stayed home," he mumbled as his eyes closed against his will. He drifted off to sleep. In his dreams he saw Grace asking him to come save her.

Grace awoke in the early morning hours and yelled out softly, "Is any one there? Please…is anyone there? …Please, please answer me."

"What do you want girl?" asked the intruder coldly.

"Please, I have to go to the bathroom," said Grace in desperation.

"And…," answered the intruder.

"And…I would go where I am, but I don't know where I am and I don't want to fall into the lake or get burned again….please take me somewhere to use the bathroom," asked Grace.

"Go where you stand and just don't go back to that spot again."

"Please, if it is not a disgrace in itself to be kidnapped, please don't make me disgrace myself by going to the bathroom here…please," pleaded Grace. "I don't know how long I am going to be here and if I have to go to the bathroom at different points then I will soon have nowhere to stand but in my own waste. And if for some reason you have to come and get me…then you will have to step over that waste, and if it gets on me and you have to touch me…then….” Grace paused.

At those words the intruder proceeded towards her and walked her out of the cave to a spot where she could use the bathroom. All she could do was give a sigh of relief as she went to the bathroom. The intruder then guided her back to her prison of fire and stone. Unknown to the intruder, Grace was counting her steps and marking in her memory how to get free.

“Leader, do you think we will make it to the girl in time?” queried one of the Trackers.

“I hope so…Teams two, four, and three are headed to the other mountains to see if she is there, but I think we are on the correct path.”

“Why do you say that, cono?”

“Don’t you smell him? That young boy came this way,” recalling Dar watching them from the doorway.

“The young boy from the school?” one of the Trackers said.

"Yes his name is Dar…it smells like he has about a good ten hours in front of us," replied Leader.

"Should we inform the principal that he is out here?" another Tracker asked.

"No. It does not matter who makes it to the girl first…it just matters that someone gets to her in time."

"What do you mean 'in time,' cono?" a Tracker asked.

"Don't you smell it in the air? It smells like it is time for the Phoenix to awaken, and when that happens the entire mountain is set afire for an entire day."

"When will this take place cono?"

"I don't know, but if I can smell it this far from here then my answer is soon."

'Go Dar, please make it to her in time,' Leader thought.

Dar jerked awake. He looked out of his little hut toward the sky that was not yet touched by the rays of the morning sun. Still lying on his back, he cautiously attempted to move his legs which, to his great surprise, beckoned to his call. Slowly he sat up and brushed the grass and dirt out of his hair. When he lowered the shelter around him, he stood and stretched his body only to buckle over in pain.

Repositioning himself back on the ground to give his body some time to wake up and rest a little longer, he gathered some berries that were close by. "I have to make it to the mountain before the Trackers do….who knows what Eres and his crew will do if they find her before I do? There must be a quicker way to the mountain," he said before he put a handful of berries in his mouth.

After some time, Dar got up and started walking in the direction of the mountain. He knew that his body was not fully recovered enough to run a long distance. But he also knew that at this pace he would not make it in time to Grace. He was in a conundrum that he could not see his way out of, until an idea flashed across his mind.

"I will fly. I have not perfected it yet, but it can still cut some miles off my trip. And take some stress off my body."

He swirled his arms in a circle, causing air currents to form around each arm. When he had concluded that he had gathered enough air, he started a light jog. He could feel the burning raise up in his legs, but he ignored it as he started to flap his arms like a bird.

Before long, he started to lift up off the ground only to crash seconds later. "Vipers-pit," Dar said as he hit his fist against the ground.

He got up and tried three more times. "I can't waste any more time on this," he said as he got up and stubbornly started to walk towards the mountain again.

Thinking on why it did not work he caught a glimpse of something outside the corner of his eye, sparking an idea.

He took off running and instead of forming the wind around his arms he formed it underneath his body and surfed on that wind current, similar to a leaf floating along on a breeze. Lifting higher into the air, Dar soon found himself looking down at the tree tops below him.

Not before long, he started to see the peak of Fire Mountain in the distance. He could smell the ash and sulfur emanating from the fiery mountain, so close now that he could feel the heat pulsating from it.

"It is so hot...," he said when he came to the base of the mountain. Thinking where he should begin, he just started yelling Grace's name.

Hearing the muffled call of her name, Grace yelled, "I am here! I am here!" However, her screams could not be heard over the erupting steam vents.

"I have to get out of here or else they will not find me," she said.

"Okay, it is about one thousand two hundred and twenty-eight steps to the exit…that man had me walk in front of him…so that must mean the walkway is narrow….God please help me to make it across this pit safely….here goes." She placed one foot in front of the other once she located the narrow strip. Realizing quickly that she could not make it across if she walked, she got down on her hands and knees and felt her way down the narrow path.

The intruder watched as she crawled across the walkway and commented to himself, 'Smart girl.'

Crawling, she could still hear her muffled name being called. However, whenever she tried to yell she would lose her balance, so she decided to keep quiet until she reached the exit. When she finally felt that the ground was wider underneath her body, she got up and started to walk towards the exit.

"I believe it was about fifty steps to the exit," she said as she counted carefully.

When she reached the exit, she now could hear her name being called much clearer. She recognized the voice to be Dar's, and with all her might she yelled out his name.

When he heard his name he came to a sudden stop and started to run in the direction of her voice. "Call my name, Grace! Call my name!"

She continued to scream his name until she saw his light approaching her. Seeing him clearly now, she ran towards him yelling his name with tears streaming down her face.

Dar watched as she ran toward him with all of her strength. All he could do was pause and open his arms to receive her. She hit him so hard that they both fell on the rough stones, sliding down the mountain side.

When they came to a stop Grace said through tears, "Dar I was so afraid…I…I…was so afraid. You did not come yesterday and I thought you would never come. And – And I know it is not your responsibility to look after me. But I hoped and I prayed and here you are."

"I will always come for you Grace," Dar said while stroking her hair, surprised by the words he just declared. "But we have to go…we still have to make the trip back down the mountain."

Grace dried her tears and nodded as the mountain began to suddenly shake and fire started to erupt out of the mountain.

"Don't be afraid Grace…I am here and I will protect you," Dar said as he felt her body stiffen against his.

"What is it? An earthquake?"

"No. The Phoenix is waking up," he replied looking towards the top of the mountain. "Come, Grace I must get you out of here," he said as he grabbed her by the hand and ran down the mountain.

They tripped on several sharp fire stones and Grace cut her knees badly. Her night gown was soaked in the blood coming from her knees. But the urgency for them to get off the mountain prevented her from shedding a tear.

When they arrived at the base Dar turned to her. "I will be right back."

"Where are you going, Dar?" Grace said in a panicked voice.

"To finish my mission."

"Don't be foolish!" she said angrily, then pleaded "please don't leave me."

"I must."

He ran off using the wind to sweep him up to the nest of the Phoenix. When he arrived at the entrance of the Phoenix's cave he took a deep breath and proceeded slowly towards the creature. He noticed that it was moving but its eyes were not yet open.

When he approached the creature he ran his hand slowly along the feathers which looked like they were on fire, but they did not burn him. He watched as the creature moved his fiery red beak to its seven-inch claws as if in the process of cleaning them in its sleep.

Reaching the tail feathers he pulled one, still keeping his eyes on the bird. He pulled another, and another, until he had four feathers. As he turned around to walk out, there was a sudden explosion and he was knocked unconscious to the ground.

When he came to, standing over him was the Phoenix. He lay paralyzed with fear looking into the golden eyes of this great bird. However, the Phoenix did not attack. It stared at him as though it knew him from somewhere. After a few moments, the bird turned its back and walked away.

Still paralyzed, Dar did not move until the mountain started to crack underneath him. Then he slowly got up and backed out of the Phoenix's dwelling. When he got outside he flew on a current of wind back to Grace.

"Let's go," Dar said, grabbing Grace by her hand.

Walking away he looked back at the mountain which was on fire from the very base to the very peak.

"Why are you so quiet?" Grace finally asked.

"I am just grateful to have found you," he replied, looking at the mountain. "I told you it was dangerous to be around me. But there is nothing I can do about it now. My plan failed."

"Very much so," she said weakly, taking a deep breath as they began to walk.

Within an hour of their departure, Grace collapsed to the ground. "I can't go on any further Dar...I made it this far...but I am in too much pain."

"Let me see your knees, Grace," Dar said.

Grace sat down on the ground and pulled up her blood-soaked nightgown to let Dar examine her knees. When he touched her knees she shrieked in pain. "I am sorry, Grace," he said.

"That is okay."

"It looks bad and the sun is setting. I will do what I can, but I need you to be strong. I am going to get some water to clean your cuts with...I will be right back," he said as he ran to a nearby stream and gathered up some water in a sack. When he returned he poured it over her knees.

Grace wanted to scream in pain, she wanted to shout out for mercy, as he was cleaning her cuts, but she held it in. Dar could see the streams of tears running down her face as he was bandaging her knees with pieces of her ripped nightgown.

"There…all done," he said in a gentle voice.

"Thank God," replied Grace as she fell back on the plush grass.

"Dar…" Grace said softly as she wiped away the tears.

"Yes."

"Did you see anyone else on the mountain?"

"No, I did not."

"Do you think he will come for me again?"

"No," Dar replied looking at the feathers in his hand.

"How do you know?"

"Because he would never have let you leave."

"I under…," she was saying as her stomach started to growl.

"It sounds like you are hungry."

Grace sat up, faced Dar, and smiled weakly as the last tear dropped from her eyes, "Yes I am."

"I will go get you something," he said as he got up to collect some wild fruits and plant roots.

When he came back he found her fast asleep on the ground curled up. He quietly made a small camp fire and formed a hut over her. When he crawled into the hut he sat down next to her and watched her sleep. This reminded him of the first time that they met in the Whispering Woods. Sighing deeply to himself, he laid down next to Grace in the small shelter as he thought about the long walk back to school. However, their rest was short-lived as they were soon awoken by rustling in the woods.

"What is it Dar?"

"I don't know, but come close to me," he said as Grace crawled slowly over to him.

He grabbed her by the hand and guided her outside of the hut, saying softly, "We may have to run, Grace."

She shuddered at the thought, as she touched her knees, and hoped for the best. Dar turned around and was about to run when a voice called out to him, "Don't move, Dar Augustus!"

"Who is there?" demanded Dar.

Out of the shadows of the night, the Trackers emerged from the woods. "You can call me Leader," a black and brown Ivoro spoke out.

"You are the Trackers hired by Principal Zarena," replied Dar.

"We are. And it looks like you have found the lost girl," Leader said looking at the bloody little girl in her tattered night gown hiding behind Dar.

When she heard the Trackers' voices she fell to the ground unconscious.

Looking at Leader Dar asked, "Can you help her? She really hurt her knees when we were coming off of Fire Mountain."

"Bring me a light," Leader said to one of his comrades.

"I see…her knees are infected but it is treatable with a few balms. It is not as bad as it looks, but it is very painful. I am surprised she did not pass out a long time ago. This is a strong girl."

"I know," Dar said, looking at her.

While she lay unconscious, Leader stitched her wounds closed and placed special balm over her knees.

"We will leave early in the morning to return to the school. She will be okay and she should not be in any more pain when she wakes up," Leader said to Dar.

"Can I stay with her?" Dar asked.

"Yes you can, but don't wake her up. You and she can have that tent over there," Leader said, pointing to a little tent in the distance set up by Leader's aide. He had earlier observed Dar's hut and found it wanting. Dar slowly picked up Grace, and carried her into the tent. As he laid her down he lay next to her so his face was facing hers.

After a few hours, he fell asleep, only to be awoken by Grace. "Dar. Dar, wake up," she said softly.

"What is it Grace? Is something wrong?" Dar said, rubbing his eyes.

"Yes, I can't feel my knees," Grace said in a panic.

"Don't worry, it is the medicine. They put a special balm on your knees. I guess it makes your knees numb so that you don't feel any pain," replied Dar.

"Oh." Dar could hear the relief in her voice.

"How much longer until sunrise?" asked Grace.

"We still have a while, about five hours," replied Dar. "Go back to sleep," he said, turning on his side.

"Dar, may I ask you a question?" she said laying back down.

"Sure, what is it Grace?" he said, turning towards her.

"Before I woke you up…you were crying in your sleep. You kept on saying 'It is all my fault, it is all my fault.' What were you dreaming about?"

Dar turned away from her and said, "Nothing," as he got up, and walked out of the tent. Grace followed him and grabbed his shoulder. When he turned around, she felt a tear hit her hand. "I am sorry Dar…I did not mean to intrude."

"It is not you Grace," Dar said, unable to hide the little sob in his throat.

"What is the matter then?"

"This is not the night to tell such a story…let's go back," he said as he took Grace by her hand.

When he saw Leader waving him over he instructed Grace to go on in and get some rest and he would be there shortly. After she went into the tent he walked over and sat next to Leader on the ground. "Do you think all great people become stars?" Leader said looking up into the night sky.

"Well cono, I don't know," replied Dar, looking up. "I hope so."

"Do you see that star over there? …I believe that is my friend who died two years ago…and that one over there is my friend who died fifteen years ago."

"Why would they become stars, cono?" asked Dar, still looking up at the jet black sky.

"So that whenever someone misses them, all they have to do is look up and it is like they never left."

Leader stood up, placed his hands behind his back, and looked up at two bright stars in the middle of the sky. "What do you think of those two stars there?" Leader asked Dar.

Dar stood up with him and looked at the two stars, "It looks like they are holding hands…don't they Cono Leader?"

"Just call me Leader. Put the formalities to the side," he said.

He then looked back up at the stars and said, "You are right they certainly do, don't they."

"Are they your friends too?" asked Dar.

"Two of my greatest friends," he said.

"What were their names?"

"Their names were Dious and Aurora Augustus," said Leader, looking down at Dar. Dar peered back at him through wide eyes.

"You knew my parents?" Dar said slowly.

"I did."

Dar put his head down and said softly, "Then you know it is all my fault that they are dead."

"This is what I know. I know that a loving father and a loving mother fought to save a son that they loved. Fault...I know no fault in that."

"If I had stayed at home…then…then…."

"If you keep looking at the if's in life you will never live," said Leader. He then faced Dar, put his hands on his shoulders, and said, "I know your parents would not want you to live with this guilt," he ended as he left.

When Dar felt he was a distance away, he beckoned to the call of his body as he clasped his knees. Looking up at the stars, as they became blurry through his tears, he bellowed, "How could you forgive me? It is all my fault!"

At the sound of the pain in Dar's voice, Grace got up and came over to him. She recognized that same voice as her own when her mother died. She bent down on her knees and gathered Dar's head into her chest where he just cried. Dar wrapped his arms around her.

Both Dar and Grace were found the next morning wrapped in each other arms with tear stains down their faces. The troops just looked at each other and at the kids on the ground. "What are you waiting for?" Leader said, "Wake them up it is time to go."

Upon awakening they got up, but they did not say a word to one another. They did not speak to each other even when they entered the campus the following day.

"Grace and Dar, I am so happy you two are safe," replied La'Sia, hugging them both.

"Dar, why did you leave campus without permission?" scolded the principal.

"I asked him to come because of his connection with the girl," Leader quickly spoke up, catching both Dar and the principal off guard.

"Well Cono Leader, next time please inform me when you are taking one of my students off campus, but forgive me....welcome back Dar and Grace. I am happy you two are both safe…, even though you are a little banged up from your trip. Please, Cona La'Sia, take Grace. Dar please go to your room for some rest after checking in with the nurse," ordered the principal.

When the children were gone the principal turned to Leader, "Did you find out who took Grace?"

"No, they hid their scent from us when we got too close."

"What if they do it again?"

"Then you know where to find me…I will not be far," he replied as he took her hand. "Good day Pilla."

"Good day Leader."

As Dar walked back to his room he looked up at the early morning sky. The sun was now kissing the horizon with its beams. He paused for a moment and looked at the morning mist rising from the ground. He said softly, "I am home again."

As he continued to walk he came across Eres, Leo, and Altis waiting outside of his dormitory. Altis was sitting on the gray stone wall that Leo was leaning against. Eres stood in the middle of the walkway and said, "Well…look boys who made it back and look…" he said slowly, "He looks a little hurt. This one was not as easy as the Varcus' challenge, huh, second year?"

Altis jumped off of the wall. "You're right Eres, the poor second year looks broken." Then he walked over to Dar who stopped in his tracks. "Do you have something for us? Today is the night of the seventh moon."

Dar reached into his back pocket and took out three of the feathers from the tail of the Phoenix. Leo quickly came over, took the feathers out of his hand, and gave them to Eres.

"That is a good boy," Altis said, as he patted Dar on the head.

Leo gave Eres the feathers, and Eres immediately engulfed them in a ball of fire. "Ooops…did I do that? All that work…gone."

The three boys laughed at Eres' comment, but Dar never looked into their eyes. He did not care to see their eyes, and he did not care that the feathers were lost. He was just happy that Grace was safe.

Dar walked passed the cloud of smoke and the laughing boys towards his dorm room, but he suddenly stopped. Boldness rose up in his chest and he peered over his shoulder smugly declaring, "Finally a dare worth doing."

"Arrogant snake," Leo spit at him.

"Arrogance is all he has right now," Eres said as he looked at Dar walk away.

Chapter Eight

My Past Revealed

The coolness of the summer night was still in the air when Dar awoke to the chiming of the school bell. He rolled on his side and looked out his window as a cloud danced across the moon.

"It's 8 o'clock," he mumbled drowsily as he sat up.

'Tonight is the gala,' he paused at the thought.

As he stood up his body cried with pain, recalling its fall down the mountain. He rubbed his legs and shoulders as he pulled all of his blankets off the bed, and threw them in the corner.

"I can't believe I got my blankets so dirty and bloody," he said looking at the soiled sheets in the corner on his way towards the washroom.

Before he got into the shower he filled the shower basin with warm water. When he got in, he pulled the rope allowing the warm water to run over his head and down his body for a few moments as he thought of how lucky he was to be alive. He watched the dirt and soot run down to his feet and out a man-made hole to the river.

Looking up he murmured slowly, "Leader, how could you know?" but he quickly shook away those thoughts and pulled the string to stop the water.

He stood there for a moment and watched a lonely tear drop to the shower floor as thoughts of his parents skipped across his mind. Thoughts of what was and what could have been, but the trance was broken when he heard someone enter the shower stall next to him.

With a soft sigh he got out of the shower, got dressed, and walked towards La'Sia's house.

When he arrived at her door, before he could even knock, the door was opened. Standing in the doorway was Grace, all washed and dressed in a pink dress. She had on lavender boots, and her hair was pulled and braided in a tight ponytail.

"You saw me coming?" Dar asked her.

"I did."

"I came over to see if you were up to going to the gala tonight. It is about quarter after nine and the gala is not over until midnight."

"Aren't you tired? You had a long day," Grace said with a little worry in her voice.

"A little," he replied. After a pause he looked at the ground and said softly, "I am sorry that I did not speak to you on the trip back here. It was nothing you did."

"You don't need to apologize. I understand when people need time to themselves."

"Dar, it is nice to see you," La'Sia said when she entered the room to see the two youth standing in the doorway.

"Dar asked me to the gala."

Pausing, La'Sia said nothing as she cautiously chose her words, "I'll walk you down."

When they arrived at the building she said in a kind voice so that Grace would not pick-up on how stern and worried her face looked, "Dar...please take good care of her. She is in your charge."

"I will cona," said Dar with a nod that soothed some of her discomfort.

"Are you going to come back for us?" Grace asked.

"No dear. There will be enough people leaving at once," she said as she walked away.

"Cona La'Sia told me she had to throw away that nightgown of mine," Grace said breaking the silence between them when she left. "She said that it was beyond hope."

"If you could have seen that nightgown I believe you would have said the same thing. I had to use a good portion of it to create those bandages for you."

"My knees were on fire…I remember when I was in that place I just stopped moving, because I got sick of getting burned," she said as she pointed to several burn spots on her arms and her legs.

"Well, I am glad you are safe," he said as he entered the building accidentally hitting Aphreneea with the bronze door.

"Aphreneea, I am so sorry. How – how are you?" he stumbled as he helped her to her feet.

"I am okay, but I cannot say the same about you," she said looking at him up and down. "You look horrible…how did you get so bruised?"

"I had a bad fall."

"I would say so."

"Who did you come with?" he asked trying to take the attention off of his cuts and bruises.

Aphreneea sighed and said, "Mikos Semaja."

"You are here with Mikos…I thought he would be the last one you would ever come here with."

"I thought so too, but when he asked me shaking and nervous….I just said yes. It was kind of sweet how nervous he was," Aphreneea said while dusting off a couple of cookie crumbs from her green ankle length dress. "And look who you have brought with you," she said looking at Grace, "Nice to see you again."

"You too…in a sense."

"Well, come on over we still have two empty seats at our table," Aphreneea said while summoning them with her hand to follow her.

"Come on Grace, let's go."

When they came to the table they were greeted by Ren and her date, and Mikos, who had just returned from getting Aphreneea a drink.

"Hello Dar," a thin brown-eyed, blond haired boy said.

"Hey Mikos, it is nice to see you," Dar replied as he pulled out a seat for Grace. He then turned to Grace and said, "Would you like anything?"

"Something to drink, please."

"How did you do it?" Ren whispered as she watched Dar go off to get her drink.

"Do what?" Grace replied.

"How did you soften him? Dar is a nice fellow but I have never seen him this nice to anyone," replied Ren a little louder.

"I think you are over-thinking things," Ren's date announced as he tuned into their conversation.

"I am not I see it in his eyes."

"I guess…it is because I can't see," answered Grace.

"No, that is not it," interjected Aphreneea, "that is not it at all."

Grace faced in the direction of Aphreneea's voice and said, "What do you mean?" But Aphreneea did not answer as Dar returned with two cups of juice.

"Here you go Grace…I hope you like Jasper juice."

When she sipped a little of the juice, she found out that she did not like Jasper juice at all. Her facial expressions gave away her distaste.

"You don't like it," Ren said.

"Oh…it is not bad…it is just an acquired taste," she said taking another sip.

"If you don't like it Grace you do not have to drink it."

"Oh…no…no…I like it."

"Grace, you are such a bad liar," Aphreneea said, which made everyone laugh.

"I can't stand Jasper juice either," Mikos said. "To me…a slug-skunk's mucus would taste better."

"I don't think it is that bad, Mikos," Aphreneea said.

Mikos got up and bowed before Aphreneea, while holding out his tawny beige hand, "To each his own my dear, may I have the honor of this dance."

"You may," Aphreneea said, taking Mikos' out stretched hand.

Soon following Aphreneea and Mikos, Ren and her date went to the dance floor. Dar looked at Grace, who steadily looked towards the dance floor. He took her by the hand and led her to the dance floor. By the time they reached the candle lit floor, the high paced music changed over to a soft mellow tone.

Dar took Grace, drew her close to him, and started to dance. She laid her head against his chest and she listened to the gradual increase in his heart until she sensed that he began to pull away. Slightly closing the gap, they danced in unison until the music ended and they left the dance floor.

When they went back to the table the three couples laughed for the rest of the night, and told great stories until the clock sounded that it was midnight and the gala ended.

"I'll walk you home Grace," Aphreneea said.

"No, no, I got it Aphreneea," Dar interjected, as Cona La'Sia's face came across his mind.

"Well…it's your choice, let's go Mikos."

"Good night everyone. See you on the next school day," said Grace as she waved goodbye to them as she left the dance hall.

"Tonight was perfect Dar. Thank you for inviting me."

"I am happy you enjoyed yourself," he said smiling.

When they returned to La'Sia's house they did not immediately go inside. They sat down together on the stone steps in front of the house.

"I never ever thought I would be in a place like this ever," said Grace looking up at the night sky.

"Do you want to go home?"

"I do. But I don't. I have no one at home who really loves me, except my friend Julia. My mom died in an accident trying to save me and my dad got sick of consumption and he died. My aunt took me in, but I hate it there and I hate her. I am sorry 'hate' is such a strong word…I dislike her to the extent that you can dislike anyone. She treats me like a dog, she calls me names, she belittles me every day, and I am just tired of her. Sometimes I wish that I died with my mother. But you know what Dar? For the first time in my life I am happy that I did not, because I would have never met Cona La'Sia, Principal Zarena, Aphreneea, Siren, and you," she said, looking at Dar.

"Well, I am happy that your wish was not granted," Dar said as he placed his hand on her knees, "How do your legs feel?"

"Much better."

"Well, it is getting late…I believe that you should go inside."

"But I am not yet tired," Grace said grabbing his hand when he got up to leave. "Are you tired, Dar?"

"To tell you the honest truth, I am not. Would you like to go for a short walk?"

Grace popped up and nodded her head.

"I know a good spot," he said taking her by the hand.

As they walked through the school campus Dar noticed that Grace kept on looking at him. When he could not take it any longer he said, "Do you have a question Grace?"

"I do…but," she paused.

"But…what?" he said.

"But I am afraid of how you will react."

"Well, ask me and we shall see."

"While in the woods you were crying in your sleep, and you told me that your story was not a story to be told on such a night…what is your story Dar?"

Dar stopped. "My story….do you really want to hear it?"

Grace nodded as he guided her to a nearby bench.

"This happened about eight years ago. My father and I went out hunting in the woods as we normally do. Our woods are full of many animals…It's nothing like the Whispering Woods. There are trees that stretch to the very heavens. The grass is always golden and green in color. And there is this special flower called the Lover's Flower, which is all white down to the stem and leaves. It grows everywhere. I loved going hunting with my father; ever since the day that I could walk I went hunting with him – learning the tricks of the trade. However, this particular day would change my life forever."

"When my father and I came to our normal hunting grounds we came to a shocking sight. If you could see it Grace, you would wish to be blind. That image I cannot erase from my mind. It was horrible. All across the ground where dead bodies. Not whole dead bodies, but pieces of dead bodies. I believe if I could have put them all together, there would have been about thirty Travelers. Their heads were in one place, while their arms were in another place, and…"

Grace interjected, "How do you know that they were Travelers?"

"Because all Travelers are born with a diamond shaped birth-mark on their foreheads."

"When we came across them, only one Traveler was still alive…he was wounded to the point of death. I remember him so clearly as if he was standing before me right now. His eyes were green and his skin brown. He had short green hair that was dyed slightly red by the blood coming out of his head. He was a young man."

"And whenever he tried to speak blood would ooze out of his mouth – it was displeasing to watch. So I remember that I turned my head from him, but when I did that is when I saw out of the corner of my eye a creature that I have never seen before. I did not get a good look at it, because it moved so fast. My father saw the creature too, and he immediately put up giant walls of earth around us and the Traveler. When he reached the Traveler he took him underneath his arms. He told me that we were going to have to run as fast as we could. He told me to get on his back – which I did. When I climbed up, all I could hear the Traveler say was, "There is no hope; we are all going to die.""

"When my father took off running he put up walls of earth and stone to slow the creature down."

"But you never saw the creature," questioned Grace.

"No…you are wrong…I eventually did see the creature for a brief moment, if calling it a creature is even the word to describe it…I saw death in that creature. And I guess my father saw the same thing. The Traveler urged my father to put him down, because he was slowing us down, but my father refused his request. You have to know my father would not leave anyone to their death."

"But somehow the Traveler managed to get out of my father's arms and he fell to the ground. I saw him roll further towards the creature as my father continued to run. You could hear his screams of pain as the creature got a hold of him."

"Did you see the Traveler die?" asked Grace.

"No, I did not, but such screams could only lead to one end. My father knew that it was too late for him so that is why I believe that he continued to run. But soon the creature was catching up with us. My father told me that he was going to put me down and that I must run as fast as I can home to mother. I told him that I did not want to leave him, but he would hear none of it. He said that he would be okay."

"So when he put me down I ran home as fast as I could. When I got home I told my mother that father was fighting some type of creature two miles down the hunting trail. She told me not to leave the house and she ran out after him. I watched her run down the stony dirt path between the towering rows of trees that lined the path. I waited in the house for a few minutes and then I followed her."

"When I came to the battleground and saw my parents battling with the creature - they were amazing. They were great Elementers. They fought long and hard. But during the battle this creature caught a glimpse of me in the bushes. I heard my mother yell 'Run!' I ran so hard and so fast, but it caught me, and when it was about to kill me my mother came over and used her body as a shield for me."

"I can still see her blood rising into the air and splashing on my face. I can still hear her screams of pain. My father came over as the beast jumped into the air and out of sight. He looked at her. I could see that he was in great anguish. When he reached down to pick me up the beast suddenly reappeared and slaughtered my father. Such a sight a child should never see. It happened so fast."

"I stood over my dead parents on the ground, covered in their blood, their eyes still opened wide. I can still see them Grace…looking at me. I have nightmares of their eyes Grace," he said as he pushed down a sob. "If it weren't for me my parents would still be alive. They died trying to save me. If I had stayed at home like my mother told me…they would not be dead. It is all my fault, it is my fault that they are dead."

"And you want to know the worst part about it? I don't know how I survived. I don't know what happened to the creature. I don't know how I got back home. I don't know why I am alive."

"But you are alive, Dar," Grace said putting her arms around him. "You are alive. You cannot blame yourself for their deaths. I know that they don't blame you."

"How do you know this Grace?" said Dar fighting back tears.

"Because they died loving you. They did not want to see their only son killed, but there is nothing I can really say to make you feel better, but to say it is not your fault."

"Thank you Grace," Dar said quietly as he listened to the bell chime that it was now one o'clock in the morning, "But I know the truth…and I have come to terms with it…I better get you home before Cona La'Sia thinks something has happened again."

Grace nodded her head, but thought to herself, 'You have not come to terms with it, Dar.'

When they came back to La'Sia's home he waited in the garden until he could see her silhouette in her bedroom window. He watched her for a few moments moving from one side of the room to another, and then departed for his dorm room.

Chapter Nine

A Garden of Sorrow

The days following their return from Fire Mountain passed so quickly for Dar and Grace. Dar came over and visited with her every moment he had. Grace never knew such joy existed outside of her friendship with Julia. She came home to the warmth of La'Sia's home and her hospitality. There was never a moment where she could not sense that La'Sia was smiling.

Even Aphreneea and Ren came to visit with her a couple of times. However, all they ever talked about each time was the boys they thought were cute on campus. Dar, in their opinion, was at the top of the list.

Grace curled up in her floral quilt and reminisced about their conversations. "I think Danos is so cute...I love his curly hair and his eyes are to die for, don't you think Aphreneea?" asked Ren, who was lying across the floral quilt on Grace's bed, looking down at Aphreneea.

"Danos is alright, but what about Antticiqious? ...he is so handsome with his jet black hair and blue eyes," Aphreneea answered, looking up at her sister. She then turned to Grace who was sitting next to her and said, "What do you search for in boys, Grace?"

"Well, sure enough it is not their looks."

"But you have a sure looker in Dar…my goodness those burnt orange eyes," Ren said.

"What is it with you and eyes Ren," Aphreneea interjected.

"I don't look at Dar that way…we are just friends," replied Grace.

"How long have you known Dar?" Ren asked Grace.

"For a long time, since we were babies," Grace answered wishing that she did not give up that last bit of information.

"I see…so he is like a best friend to you then," said Aphreneea.

"You can say that," replied Grace with a smile.

"Humph…well…I feel sorry that you feel that way…you two would make a good couple," replied Ren.

"Ren…sometimes the very person you see as a best friend can one day become so much more," Aphreneea responded as they got up to get ready for the next day.

Aphreneea's words rang in Grace's ears as she sat up when Cona La'Sia knocked at her door. "Come in," Grace said.

"Are you still in bed Grace?" La'Sia said when she entered the room.

"I was just thinking about this past week…that's all."

La'Sia came over and sat on the edge of her bed. "How would you describe it?"

"It was enjoyable. It was perfect."

"I am so glad to hear that. I am also so happy that you made some nice friends so quickly," La'Sia said, getting up from the bed. "I will be leaving in five minutes to go work. Are you up to coming this dium? "

"Yes, I am," Grace said as she recalled that dium meant week. She popped out of bed and quickly dressed after La'Sia closed the door to give her some privacy.

After she quickly washed up in the bowl of water in her room, she went downstairs. In the kitchen she could hear some movement. "Good morning again Cona La'Sia," Grace said.

"Good morning, you must be Grace," a male voice responded.

"Oh, Grace, I was just coming up to get you...I see that you have met Tilo Burnos," La'Sia said, entering the kitchen and looking at the jet black haired gentleman with the almond-shaped eyes.

"Oh...Cono Burnos, it is a pleasure to meet you," said Grace, holding out her hand.

"Ummm..." was all he could muster as he looked through his burnt orange eyes at the girl's hand.

Grace had forgotten that the customs of her time were not common in this place, "Oh, I am sorry," she said withdrawing her hand; "...it aches a little." Grace shyly laughed.

"Tilo is a professor at the local university and a friend of mine," said Cona La'Sia touching his light olive skin. "He came here to talk to some of our students about college."

"That's exciting," Grace said as La'Sia guided her to an open chair, "You must be very smart."

"I guess so," Tilo said confidently as he took his seat again, "But, I never thought that I would be a professor to tell you the honest truth. I never thought that I was much of a people person."

"How could you say that?" La'Sia interjected, "There was never a moment where you were not surrounded by people. I swear," she paused as she leaned a little across the table, "you could have charmed the rattle off an akarpus and put any scholar to shame with that brain of yours. You were, are brilliant. To me people treated you like you were a god."

"Except for you, you were stubborn," he said laughing, "But tell me, what made you change your mind?"

"Well," she said leaning forward a bit more, "You were leaning against this old oak tree all alone, looking pathetic by the way, and you were just looking up at the stars; and then you began rubbing your eyes. At first I thought something fell into your eyes, until I heard a gently sob. Just a quiet one, but I guess it surprised even you, because you jumped a little and then you began looking around. But I guess you did not see me, because you went back to looking up at the stars. I don't know. It seemed at that moment that you were a person after all and that I may have judged you too soon."

"Really?" he said leaning forward, "And here I thought that my charm and grace finally won you over," he said as he patted her hand.

Pulling her hand away, she bellowed, "Not at all! At first, I wanted to have nothing to do with you. I thought you were arrogant and a bit pompous. But I am happy that I gave you a fourth chance. We had a lot of fun together at the University, even though we only had a few classes together."

"Even with those few classes and our two different career paths, our friendship never diverged," he said looking over to Grace whom he had forgotten about until she stirred.

Smiling and clearing his voice, "Well Grace, now you know how we met and why she does not hate me."

"Oh, I understand. Are…," Grace said, but was interrupted by a knock at the door. La'Sia opened the door to Dar waiting on the other side.

"Oh, Dar, it is you. How did you know Grace was coming today?" replied La'Sia.

"It was just a guess, cona. I thought since all her burns were looking better, she might want to come to school today."

"That is very insightful of you Dar, but you did not have to come and get her. I would have taken her to the office," replied La'Sia.

"It is no problem at all Cona La'Sia," replied Dar with a smile when he saw Grace coming out of the kitchen.

"But coming here is so far out of your way."

"Well, I am an early bird and it is good exercise…are you ready Grace?" Dar said never making eye contact again with La'Sia after Grace entered the room.

"Yes, I am," Grace said, walking towards that bright spherical light that made her heartbeat a little faster every time she saw it.

"I am very happy to have met you. I'm sorry I have to depart so soon," she said to Tilo as she left the kitchen.

"That is not a problem. It was nice meeting you, too. I hope to see you more often."

When they left the house Dar asked, "Who was that?"

"Oh…that is Cono Burnos. He has come from the university."

"How does Cona La'Sia know him?"

"He is her friend."

"I see…..ooohhh…before I forget, I have a present for you Grace," he said when he came to the stone circle pathway. "Stay here and I will be right back." He ran off to the nearby woods and grabbed a stick that he had carved and smoothed down. "Here you go Grace," Dar said, handing her the long stick.

"You got me a stick," Grace said rubbing her hands up and down it. "Oh…I feel carvings on it now. Did you do this yourself Dar?"

"I did."

"It is lovely," Grace said turning to give Dar a big hug as Aphreneea and Ren came up behind them.

"Best friends, huh," said Aphreneea with a smile.

"Look what Dar gave me," Grace said as she held the present out to Aphreneea, who gently took it out of her hands.

She looked at it up and down and said, "It is a divine stick. Dar, I guess professor Ruz's art class paid off," she said as she placed the stick back into Grace's hand.

"I would appreciate that you girls stop calling it a stick, for it is a rod," replied Dar with a bit of annoyance.

"We are sorry," the girls said in sequence.

"Come on, we are going to be late for school," replied Dar, taking Grace by the hand. "Come on Aphreneea and Ren, we're going to be late," turning around to the girls.

"Yeah, yeah, Dar," Aphreneea said.

When they reached the school Aphreneea and Ren separated from them, going off into their first period class.

Dar and Grace went to their History class. Once the class began Dar's teacher discussed the History of the Elementers and gave a brief introduction of the Trackers of the North Mountain:

"The Trackers of the North Mountain are courageous and bold men and women. Whenever a village is in danger they are there to help or when someone needs to be found they step up to the plate. They are noble men and women…" the teacher was saying when the bell sounded, "Ok, students we will continue our discussion of the Trackers of the North Mountain tomorrow and continue on with the Trackers of the East. Have a nice day."

"My next class is with professor Lynos. He is a nice professor, I like him," said Dar to Grace.

"Oh, I see…Dar is there a garden somewhere around here?"

"Yes, right outside of professor Lynos' window. Do you want to go to the garden?"

"Please, I just feel like being outside for a while…I promise that I will not move until you come and get me."

"Okay, come with me," Dar said as he steered her down the stone hallway to the garden exit. When they walked outside Grace said, "Do you smell that Dar …it smells so fresh. Can you describe the area to me?"

"Well, ummmm….it is a small garden," Dar started as he guided Grace around it. "The walls of the garden make up the walls of the surrounding classrooms. One side is the classroom and the other side is the garden…we are basically in a box. The stones are grayish white and rough to the touch…here feel it. There is a pond in the middle of the garden filled with fish. It is small, so you can't really drown in it. Let me see…Oh, there is only one stone bench in the whole garden. Take a seat."

Sitting she said, "Dar it sounds so lovely. Are there any flowers?"

Dar walked over to a patch of Ony flowers in the corner of the garden. "These are the only ones that grow in this garden," he said handing her the flowers.

Grace took the flowers and held them up to her nose. "How wonderful! They smell sweet."

"Hence their name Ony means sweet, but I have to get to class," he said quickly. "But I will come and get you after class," he noted as he walked towards the garden door.

When he left the garden he ran to his class and made it at the sound of the bell. "You just made it, Dar," Lynos said.

"I am sorry, cono," replied Dar.

"Have a seat," the professor said, causing him to walk quickly over to his desk. He looked out of the window to see Grace walking around the small garden. She used her rod to guide herself across the garden and around the pond. For the first few minutes of class he watched over her from the window until the professor called on the students to do a group activity.

At the end of the activity, he returned to his seat in shock and horror. There, next to Grace, was Leo, talking to her. He got up and was about to run out to her when the professor called him back.

"But cono, I have to go," pleaded Dar.

"Not until the bell rings, which is not for another twenty minutes…have a seat."

"I have to go to the bathroom," he quickly spat out.

"You are lying….take your seat."

"But profes…" Lynos cut him off in a stern voice. Dar obediently sat down in his seat and watched Leo talk to Grace. He was curious about what he was saying to her because their backs were towards him.

"Oh, excuse me, I did not know someone was out here," Leo lied as he looked at Grace. Grace just nodded at him, but did not respond to him, for she knew the voice of the boy who made Dar do those dares.

Leo came over and sat next to Grace, who shifted over a few centimeters from him. "Do you think that I am going to bite you my dear?" Leo said as he moved closer to her, until she felt his thigh against hers.

Grace was too afraid to say anything and only wished for Dar to come and get her. But she mustered up the courage and said, "What do you want?"

"Nothing…just to talk to you. I just want to get to know the girl who is the friend of my dear friend Dar."

"Dar is not your friend," Grace said boldly.

"Feisty aren't you? That spirit of yours could get you in trouble one day…little girl," Leo said, touching her knee which caused Grace to wince in pain. "Oh, did I hurt you?" Leo said, pressing down hard on her knee. She let out a scream that echoed up the walls of the garden.

When Dar heard her cry he burned with rage and rushed out of the room. Reaching the garden door, he pulled it open with such force that the door was knocked off of one of its hinges.

He created a whirlwind around Leo and threw him to the opposite side of the garden, where he pinned him against the stone wall by having the wall enclose around his torso.

"Don't you ever touch her again!" Dar yelled at Leo.

Leo laughed at Dar for a few minutes and then said in an ominous voice, "Who do you think you are playing with, second year?" as he began to transform his body.

Dar watched as Leo got bigger and bigger, before muttering, "A dragon."

"I am boy, and I am going to eat you alive," Leo's voice deepened as he completed his metamorphosis.

As he was about to attack, Eres appeared, leaning against the door post of the unhinged door. With his arms folded across his chest he said, "Settle down Leo, this is not the time."

"Aww, Eres….I am just having a little fun." He transformed back into his original appearance allowing his skin to take on the appearance of the clothes he ripped off.

"This is not the time, nor the place to have 'a little fun,'" he mocked Leo. "Too many eyes," he said pointing at the windows.

Leo looked up and around him, seeing all of the students and the teachers looking out of their windows at the commotion in the garden.

"Let's go Leo," Eres said as the principal came up behind him.

"Yes, let's go to the office, all of you," she said. Eres shrugged his shoulders and walked toward the office with Leo, Dar, and Grace following behind.

When they reached her office, the principal closed the door behind them and said, "There is to be no fighting in my school whatsoever. Your actions today are unacceptable, and I do not want to see it again. Do I make myself clear?"

All of the students said "yes cona" simultaneously. "Get to class now," she said firmly to Leo and Eres. She then turned to Dar and Grace, "You two, stay!"

When Eres and Leo were out of the room, Principal Zarena chastised Dar and Grace for being careless.

"Why were you in the garden by yourself, Grace?"

"To enjoy the outside, that's all," answered Grace.

"While you are in this school you are to be with Dar at every moment of the day, do you hear me?!"

"Why are you being so strict? You are treating her like she is in prison," Dar said, taking up for Grace.

"It has to be this way until we find out who took her. If you have any clues please feel free to tell me…since you were able to find her so easily," she said, sitting back in her brown leather chair with her arms folded.

"I don't, cona," replied Dar softly.

The principal then sat up in her chair and said, "Of course you don't," sarcastically. "Go on to lunch," she said to Dar and Grace.

When they were out of ear shot of the principal Grace turned to Dar angrily, "Why did you not tell her?"

"How can I?" Dar said defeated. "That will make things worse for you while you are here. They will find a way to hurt you again," he said looking at her knees.

"Again?"

"They did not say it in so many words, but it was them who kidnapped you and took you to Fire Mountain, to make sure that I kept the dare."

"But it was not them. I could tell by their voices. That intruder fellow did not have any of their voices," answered Grace as she thought back on the intruder.

"They probably hired someone," he said. "Please, Grace, get away from me. I am just trouble for you."

"Do you really think that will cause them to leave me alone? They see me as your weakness, your Achilles' heel. Plus we tried the stay away plan already."

When they reached the cafeteria, Dar turned to Grace and said, "I will tell, come on let's go."

They turned to go back to the principal's office as Eres stepped around the corner. "Where are you going?"

"To my locker," replied Dar.

"Liar!" Altis said to him, as he walked up behind him and shoved him on the shoulder.

"You fool! What did I tell you will happen if you told?" Eres said, walking toward him.

"I wasn't going to say anything, I am just going to my locker," Dar answered while positioning Grace behind him so her back was now against the gray stone walls of the hallway.

"You better not," said Altis.

"Or else your life and hers will get much, much worse," said Leo looking at Grace.

"I wasn't going to say anything, I swear to you," said Dar trying to be as convincing as possible.

"Let me remind you, second year, that these walls have ears," said Eres as he stretched out his arms to the surrounding walls. He then leaned in to Dar and whispered, "I know everything."

"Eres….I…." Dar began but was abruptly cut off.

"There is nothing more to be said here," Eres said, rising back up into an upright position. He then turned to Leo and Altis and said, "Let's go."

As he started to walk down the hallway, Leo turned around and mouthed, "Much worse."

"Come on Grace, let's go," Dar said putting his arm around her shoulders and leading her towards the exit of the school.

"Where are we going Dar? Your class is in the other direction," Grace said.

"I am skipping class today and taking you home," Dar said.

Grace pushed his arm off of her and turned around. "We are not going to run. If we run today, we will be running tomorrow," Grace said boldly.

"What if they hurt you?"

"What if? What if? Always what if," Grace said as she grabbed his hand and started to walk back.

He dropped her hand and said softly, "What if?"

"Let's cross that bridge when it comes. Live in the present and not in the past."

"We learn from our past."

"Not if we always stay there, Dar," she said grabbing his hand again and moving ahead.

"Do you know where you are going?" Dar said.

"I have no idea," she said, letting him take the lead.

Chapter Ten

Just Breathe

"How long are you going to camp outside of my window? It has been two weeks now, and nothing has happened," Grace yelled out of her window to the dancing light in the garden.

"Maybe nothing has happened because I am camped outside of your window," the light answered.

"I appreciate all that you are doing, but I cannot have you outside of my window another night. I get to sleep in a warm bed while you are sleeping on the ground," she said to Dar.

"And yesterday I know you probably got soaking wet after that storm. Enough is enough."

"But…" Dar began as she cut him off.

"But nothing…I will see you tomorrow Dar…go home," she said shutting her window.

Suddenly Dar heard a tap at his bedroom door which shook him out of his daydream. "Come in."

"The girls are waiting downstairs for us…what is taking so long?" Mikos said when he entered the room.

"I was just thinking about a conversation I had with Grace three gildiums ago," replied Dar as he got up and grabbed his jacket and hat.

"Three gildiums ago? Come on Dar, live in the present. We have to go," Mikos beckoned him. "The girls are waiting for us outside and I am ready to go."

Dar laughed, "Mikos, you are acting like you have never been on a sleigh ride before."

"I never have been on a sleigh ride with a girl before. Well, I have been on sleigh rides with girls before, but not a girl that is my girl…I mean she is not my girl, my girl, as though she is property to be claimed…but she is my girl as my girlfriend. I have a girlfriend. Can you believe it Dar? Me and Aphreneea," said Mikos taking a deep breath.

"No, Mikos, I really can't believe it," replied Dar as he walked out of his room toward the staircase.

"What about you and Grace?" he said nudging him on his arm.

"What about us?"

"Well…come on."

"We are just friends…nothing more."

"Do you want it to be more?"

"Oh.…look it's the girls," Dar said, pointing to Aphreneea and Grace to avoid his question.

Grace yelled out, "Come on Dar…let's go."

Mikos turned to Dar as they approached the sleigh and whispered, "It scares me when she does that. How does she know when you are near?"

Dar shrugged his shoulder and climbed into the driver's seat. "So where are we going?" he asked.

"How about the Ice Lake?" said Aphreneea when she climbed into the back.

"What is the Ice Lake?" questioned Grace positioning herself next to Aphreneea.

"It is a lake that, regardless of how hot it is outside, it is always frozen," answered Mikos as he climbed into the driver's seat next to Dar.

"Oh…it sounds lovely," said Grace.

"Well….Ice Lake here we come," said Dar as he whipped the lashes of the reigns causing the horses to move.

"Can we go pass my dormitory so I can pick up some skates?" Aphreneea called out from the back.

Dar nodded his head when out of the corner of his eye, he watched Mikos jump out the moving sleigh making a beeline back to his dormitory. Pulling the sleigh to a stop, it was only within moments he could see Mikos pouncing through the snow with two set of skates in his hand. One of which Dar could only assume to be for him.

Taking his position next to Dar again, who gave him a chastening glance, as they tuned into Aphreneea telling Grace the story of the frozen lake.

"Legend has it that a long time ago a beautiful princess and a handsome prince were deeply in love. They were to be married, but her dear prince had to go off to war. While in a raging battle he was fatally wounded and he died. It is said that at the moment of his death the princess felt her heart grow cold. She feared at that moment that her one dear beloved prince was dead. When the news reached the princess of his death she too died," Aphreneea paused when she came to her dormitory.

Upon her return, she continued the story as though she never left, "As was tradition, the bodies of all royal members during that time were to be burned upon their death. So they placed her body in a little wooden boat filled with straw and it was set on fire. They pushed the boat out into the lake. The boat traveled on the lake until it reached the middle were it sprung a leak and sunk. Legend has it that when her body hit the water and sunk that the lake became ice and it has been that way to this day," Aphreneea concluded.

"Hence the name Ice Lake," added Dar.

"How sad, but how romantic," replied Grace. "My friend Julia back home was reading me a story of these two lovers named Romeo and Juliet."

"What is their story?" asked Aphreneea.

"I don't know, she never had the chance to finish telling me," Grace said as she remembered that was the day she came to this realm.

"Well, you can find out when you go back home, and then you can write and tell me what their story is," replied Aphreneea jubilantly.

"Yeah…when I go back home," Grace said solemnly as she whispered, "It has already been three months."

"Look, there is the lake up there," Dar said trying to take the attention off of Grace.

In the distance, through the down-turned trees overpowered by ice and snow, was the glistening lake. "Oh...I see it!" Aphreneea said. "I love this lake, but I have not been here in ages."

"Let's go ice skating," said Mikos when the sleigh reached the lake.

"I...I...don't know how to skate on ice," replied Grace fearfully as it dawned on her that they might ask her.

"It is easy," said Aphreneea.

"I don't have any skates...I will just sit here and listen to you all and...and... nature," Grace said, trying to make up every excuse she could think of.

"Well...don't worry about that. I brought an extra pair of skates for you. You and Ren look about the same size," said Aphreneea. "Plus, Dar is an excellent skater. Aren't you Dar?"

"Well...." Dar was saying.

"Don't be shy...he is great Grace. Come on let's go. I will help you put on your skates," said Aphreneea helping her out of the sleigh.

Before she could protest, Aphreneea was taking off her boots and putting on the ice skates. "Now be careful Grace, these shoes have two blades at the bottom…but you will be safe in Dar's hands," she said with a smile. "I'll go get him for you," she said looking back at Grace who was lifting her feet up and down trying to get use to the extra weight.

When he came over she whispered, "I am afraid Dar."

"Of what?"

"Of…," she paused as a flood of memories came to her, of revealing a part of herself that she wanted to forget, "Of falling through the ice and drowning…like my mother."

"Your mother drowned by falling through thinned ice?"

"No but it was an icy night when she did drown…" she began as she took a deep inhale.

"We had just come from a friend's Christmas party. My mother and I were both singing 'Ole Saint Nick' and drinking hot cocoa when without warning the bridge started to crack. It sounded like a large branch being broken off of a tree. It was loud. The carriage buckled under us and then the bridge gave way. Within moments the carriage crashed into the ice cold lake silencing the horses. Or maybe our screams just overpowered their noise. I remember feeling the cold water sending shockwaves up my spine as my fingers were beginning to grow numb."

"My mother said to me that 'Everything is going to be okay. The shore is not that far off Grace, hold on to me tight.' She took my arms and wrapped them around her neck. When we reached the shore I heard my mother scream as her hands slipped out of mine. For a few seconds I heard clawing at the gravel before a splash."

"I remember yelling over and over again 'Mother! Mother! Answer me! Where are you?' but the only answer I got was the sound of the wind."

"All night long I sat on the shore of that river bank and cried and tried to scream, but the only thing that came out after a while was voiceless murmurs for my mother. I dared not sleep in hope of the slightest chance that she might speak."

"As the moon faded and the sun rose, I remembered being curled up in a ball to try to keep warm when the local sheriff came over to me. He asked me where my mother was.

" 'I-I-I d-d-d-d-o-o-o-o-n't k-k-k-k-n-n-now,' I babbled through shivering lips as I burst into tears that dropped across my frozen lips. 'T-t-t-he b-b-bridge b-b-broke a-n-n-d-d we b-b-b-oth m-m-m-m-ade it to to to to shore, b-b-b-b-b-ut…' I know I should not laugh, but I remember how hard it was for me to speak."

"The sheriff shushed me and told me that everything was going to be okay. He placed his coat around my shoulder and he picked some of the mud and grass out of my hair – I can only assume."

"As we got up to walk to his buggy, he stroked my arms in an attempt to make me warm when the deputy sheriff came running over. Without a second to take a breath he said, 'Sheriff I have some bad news.'"

"He beckoned the Sheriff away from me and told him that he found my mother two miles down the river dead. He thought I could not hear him, but I did. It was not until I spoke that they realized how loud they were."

"'She's dead,' I said. I was surprised that I had some control of my speech."

"My mother is dead, my father is dead, I am all alone in this world."

"'I am so sorry Grace,' the Sheriff said to me."

"When we reached the sheriff's station the town's preacher and his wife came up to me and gave me their condolences. He tried to say some sympathetic words, but I really was not listening. I just nodded my head because he was the last person I wanted to talk to about this at this time, not because he was a bad man – but, because I did not want to hear that my mother was now in a better place. I already knew that. Nevertheless, I did not want to hear it, because I wanted her to be here on Earth next to my side."

"I would not feel so bad if I could have done something about it. If I had my sight I could have done something…"

"What could you have done?" Dar said as he thought about his own situation.

"I would have saved her."

"How so?"

"I don't know – I would have done something. I was just frozen there on that shore."

"Leader told me and I will tell you the same – that if you keep looking at the "if" in life you will never live your life."

"Sometimes I feel like my life stopped the day my mother died. As though I stopped breathing, but I keep living on."

"I know the feeling."

"Then you understand that it is not something you can just get over."

"I do understand that. I have not yet gotten over the death of my parents, but I have learned to live without them. I have learned to breathe, even if it's only with shallow breaths."

"How do I start breathing again?"

"One step at a time."

"And that one step is?"

"With you, to get on that ice," he said as he gently pulled her toward the frozen lake.

"I can't," she said pulling away from him.

"I won't let anything happen to you…trust me," he said.

Taking a deep breath she nodded her head as she extended her hand.

"Sorry Dar," she said with a little nervousness when she discovered her arms were around his neck tightly as she stepped on the ice.

"That is okay," he said rubbing his neck when she let go.

He guided Grace further onto the ice and, like a baby he watched her take tiny steps in learning how to skate. No matter how many times she fell she got back up. Her determination in learning to skate shined through as a bright beacon to be admired.

For a moment, even Aphreneea and Mikos had to stop to watch her before gliding off to the other side of the lake.

 "Look, you are doing beautifully."

"Thank you," she said as she collapsed towards the ice.

"You ready to go again?" he said helping her up.

"I think I will sit out for a moment."

"Tired?"

"Bruised," she said laughing.

He led her back to the sanctuary of the shore as he went off to find Mikos and Aphreneea. She rubbed her bruises and thought of how proud her mother would be of her this day — the day that she started to breathe again.

After some time had passed, she saw Dar's light coming her way.

"How are you feeling now?"

"Much better."

"Are you ready for one more go around? Aphreneea and Mikos said they are ready to leave shortly."

"Yes, I am," she said as she wobbled to her feet.

"Look at you. You are now a pro," he was saying when she suddenly made acquaintance with the ice again.

"I would not say a pro, but I would say that I have graduated to being moderate. All thanks to you, teacher."

"You are the first, and my most crowning achievement," he said laughing as she once again greeted the ice below her feet.

Dar leaned over the giggling girl and said "Are you okay?"

Grace laughed, "Yes."

"Are you okay?" Aphreneea repeated when she came over with Mikos.

"I am okay, Aphreneea" Grace said as she got up.

"Are you sure?" said Mikos, "I think that was your worst fall of the day."

"I am sure. Don't worry about me," she said dusting the ice crystals off of her dress.

"We have been at this for some time now and my stomach is starting to note that it is about lunch time," Aphreneea remarked as she grabbed Grace's hand.

"I am starving, too. Let's go," said Mikos.

"Let's go back to campus," Aphreneea said as she guided Grace to shore.

When they arrived at the lake's edge, Aphreneea helped Grace switch back into her shoes before getting into the sleigh. Mikos helped Aphreneea into the back and Grace into the front.

"You might be more comfortable in the back than up here Grace," Dar commented.

"I'm good. Plus I think the love birds need some time to themselves," said Grace.

Mikos leaned forward between Dar and Grace and said, "It matters which ones you are talking about."

Chapter Eleven

Dear Jesus

Julia Gains
1565 Sandy Point, MD

August 17, 1878

Dear Jesus,

Hi it is me Julia. I been praying and praying for a long time now about my dear friend Grace Comings. She is a really nice girl. She is like a sister to me. But a few months ago she went missing. The Sheriff and everyone went looking for her, but no one found her. The only thing that we found was my charm bracelet I gave her. She really likes waves, so I gave her a wave bracelet. I been praying for her safe return, but maybe so many prayers are coming to you…that you do not hear my prayers. So I am writing this letter to you. My Nanna always gets my letters, so I figure if I write to my Lord he will get mine too.

Well this is my prayer. Dear Jesus, please bring back my friend Grace Comings. Jesus please bring her back safe and sound. Amen.

I know it is a short prayer, but that is all I have right now. I will write you later to make sure my letter got to you. One time my letter to Nanna got lost in the mail. So just in case this one gets lost I will send another.

Love your faithful servant,

Julia Gains

P.S. Her birthday is in one week…let her have a wonderful birthday

Chapter Twelve

The Big Day

"These last few gildiums have been very quiet," Dar said to Grace as he pushed the canoe on to the lake.

"What do you mean?"

"I have not been given one dare since the Phoenix. It has been very quiet and peaceful in my life."

"You think they are going to leave you alone?"

"Probably not, but it has been very nice. I am ahead on my school work again, which is always a good thing, and I sleep later," he said as he pushed the paddles gently through the water.

Grace sighed deeply. "What is the matter? Are you not in the mood for a canoe ride today? I can turn back around."

"It's not that. Something seems to be off today. Today is the first day I have ever felt homesick. I cannot figure out why. I've felt this way since this morning."

"You have been gone a long time?"

"Maybe? How long have I been here again?"

"I believe three gildiums."

"What is today?"

"I believe it is the twenty-fourth day of the gildium."

"What?!"

"It is the twenty-fourth day of the eighth gildium in the year," he repeated.

"I understand what you just said Dar," she paused and thought. "Today is my birthday."

"What is a 'birthday,'?" he questioned.

"It is the day you celebrate your birth."

"Today is your Mirraz Day!"

"Yes it is," she nodded while secretly adding a new word to her vocabulary.

"Then you are now fifteen today."

"I am," she said smiling and then frowning.

"Why do you look so sad on such a festive day?"

"Because this is the first birthday, Mirraz Day, that I can re-member in a long time that I am away from my friend Julia. Every year she would bake a cake for me and we would go to our secret hide-out to eat it all."

"Just the two of you, and no one else?"

"Just the two of us. It is always grand," she said.

"Now you are sad, because you don't have the cake and your friend Julia."

"A bit. But now that I think of it. I have more friends now than I ever had before. I have you, Ren, Aphreneea, and Mikos."

"Ohhh…I forgot about Mikos. I told him that I would meet him at his dormitory an hour ago. I am sorry to cut this short, but I have to go."

"It's no problem. Today Cona La'Sia and I are going to pick out the next flower of the month."

As he paddled back to shore he said, "Where does she get so many flowers from?"

"I ask her that question each month and all she would say is 'I have my ways.'"

"Sounds a little scary."

"It does," she said as she allowed Dar to help her out of the canoe.

"Here you go," he said as he handed her, her rod.

"Thank you. I guess I will see you tomorrow sometime."

"You don't want me to walk you back home?"

"I have learned my way around this campus over the last several months. I believe I can make it without getting lost."

"Okay…I will see you tomorrow," he said as Grace watched his light dance away.

However, before she started her trip back to her home she sat for a moment at the shore of the lake. She thought about the first time she met Julia Gains. It was just several days after her mother's funeral.

Like in times past, Grace found herself sitting on the beach after being chased out of her aunt's house for being a useless nobody.

"What are you doing out here?" a friendly voice asked her.

"Ohh…nothing," Grace answered while drying her tears.

"It must be something if you are crying," the friendly voice continued.

"It's nothing. Just leave me alone," Grace retorted.

"Well, I can't do that," the voice answered as the sound of someone sitting came into Grace's ears.

"What are you doing?" she questioned harshly.

"I figure if I sit here next to you and look out in the same direction you are looking – then I can find out what is making you cry."

"That is silly," Grace said as she got up to walk away.

"Where are you going?"

"Back into the house."

"Are you sure you want to do that?"

"What do you mean?"

"If I got that tongue whipping I would not want to go back into that house."

Embarrassed, Grace came back and sat down. "You heard it all?"

"I did. And I can't believe it is true. You are not useless."

"I am. I am blind and I can't do anything but get in the way," said Grace feeling the tears welling up in her eyes. "I have broken several plates and too many cups to count," she said holding out her hands to show the cuts on her hands she obtained in her attempts to clean up the glass.

"It happens," the voice said while rubbing her hands. "I once broke all of my mother's fine china and two of her best bowls within twenty seconds."

Grace laughed as she drew back her hands. "How did you do that?"

"I once read in this book about a magician who once pulled a cloth from off a table with all of the dinner dishes still on top. So I got all of my mother's china and placed it on the kitchen table and I tried it too."

"And it failed," Grace said laughing harder then she had ever done before.

"Yes, it failed. My mother came running in the room when she heard all of the commotion. When she saw what I did, she nearly collapsed on the ground. All I heard was 'Julia Samantha Gains you are in big trouble young lady.'"

"Your name is Julia."

"Ohhh…where are my manners? I have been talking to you this whole time and never told you my name. Yes, it is," the raven hair girl said.

"My name is Grace Comings."

"I know. I saw you at the funeral."

"You came over here to give some pity to the blind girl," Grace said with all the laugher gone from her voice.

"Not at all. I really did not know you were blind until this moment. I did not even know at the funeral. I thought people were holding your hand because you were sad."

"How long has your family been here?"

"Not too long," she said brushing some sand off her brown tights that matched her eyes, "My dad came here and set up our home, and mother and I came down about two months ago."

"Where are you from?"

"Virginia."

"Why would you come to Maryland?"

"Father's job sent him here. He is a banker."

"Your father is a banker. You must get a lot of things."

"I guess."

"Do you miss Virginia?"

"Not really. It is nice being in a place where no one knows who you are. It is like you get to start all over again."

"You must miss all of your friends."

"Not at all. I never had too many real friends. I knew that some of them were my friends because of who my father was and others were my friends because they thought if they were around me it would make them look better," Julia sighed as she untied the cream ribbon, that mirrored the complexion of her skin, from her hair.

"You did not have any friends at all," Grace said.

"I did have two. Their names were Beth and Sarah, but they moved away. They both moved to Europe. I got letters from them for a time, but the letters stopped coming one day."

"That is sad."

"I only expect so much from eleven year olds," she said.

"How old are you?" Grace questioned.

"Twelve, and yourself?"

"Twelve also," Grace said, and then asked, "Why did you come over today?"

"I just thought maybe you would like to come to my house and we can play," she said simply.

"With a blind girl."

"No. Just with a girl," Julia said. "Would you like to come? Or go back into the house?"

"I will come," she said without a second thought.

And from that moment on Grace remembered that Julia and she were like two peas in a pod: Always together, always laughing, and always enjoying being companions. They never complained and they never argued with each other, with the exception of the choice of novels Julia liked to read to her.

"No, Julia. Not another one. I am begging you," Grace said. "There has to be another book out there."

"Come, Grace. You have not even heard the story yet and you don't want to hear it."

"Always a love novel, Julia."

"No this time it is an epic poem…it has a lot of action in it also. I read it already and you will like it," she said.

Grace sighed, "What is the name of the book?"

"It is called The Odyssey."

"It sounds interesting."

"It is," she said gleefully. "Odysseus, the main character, is a great warrior and he has to go through all of these things to get back to his true love."

"Are you sure action is in this one?"

"Of course. You will not be disappointed, and I have something else to show you. Come with me," Julia said as she led Grace away from her house and towards the woods.

"I went on a walk yesterday and I came across this cave. It is small and quaint, but it can be our hide-out together."

"What do we call it?" Grace asked.

"I don't know. We can figure that part out later," Julia said when they arrived at the cave. "Well what do you think?" she asked as she let Grace feel her way around the cave.

"It is nice."

"Wonderful. Here take a seat and we can start the story," Julia said as she guided Grace to a stone, "There, perfect."

Grace then felt a box on her lap, "What is this?"

"Happy Birthday, Grace!" Julia yelled as she threw her hands in the air.

"What?!"

"It is August 24, 1876, happy thirteenth birthday. I made you a cake…well my mother helped me make you a cake. We can eat it together as I read to you."

"You are a sweet dear friend."

"Grace, what are you still doing here?" Dar said knocking her out of her trance.

"What?" Grace said a bit dazed.

"What are you still doing here? I went to Cona La'Sia's house and you were not there. Have you been here for an hour?"

"I don't know. I was just thinking."

"Cona La'Sia is going to have a fit if you do not go home right now. She is worried about you."

"I am sorry. I don't want her to be worried about me," she said as she got up to leave. "What are you doing?" she said to the light following her.

"Making sure you go home this time."

When they reached La'Sia's walkway Grace smelled a delightful smell and questioned Dar to what it was. Lying, he shrugged his shoulders and said, "I don't know."

When she opened the door, she heard a symphony of voices put together to say one phrase, "Blessed Mirraz Day, Grace!"

"How did you know? I just told Dar today," she said in shock.

"You may have just told Dar today, but you spoke about the day of your creation to Ren and myself a gildium ago," Aphreneea said.

"And you did all of this for me?" Grace said, moved by their compassion.

"You are far from home and we wanted to bring a little bit of home back to you," Cona La'Sia said.

"Is that why you left to get Mikos?" she asked turning to Dar.

"It was. And when you did not come we all panicked," he said. "But that is not important. Let's have some fun."

As the music was put on and the sound of different conversations filled the air, Dar walked Grace out to the back garden.

"I know this is bad timing, but I need you to do me a favor."

"Anything."

Dar leaned in and whispered into her ear. Grace nodded her head up and down in agreement. He then handed her a small package and whispered the instructions into her ear.

"Are you sure? You don't have to."

"We are friends. I can help," Grace said.

"What are you two doing out here?" Aphreneea said when she walked into the garden.

"I was just giving Grace a gift," Dar said.

"You always want to be the first," she said with a smile as she grabbed Grace's hand and walked her back into the house where they laughed and joked until the sun went down.

Chapter Thirteen

Goldings

Grace sat up quickly in her bed and the empty box Dar gave her fell to the floor. She sat for a moment in her silence as she listened to the rain pound on the window. The thunder was so loud that it sounded as though the gods themselves were fighting a furious battle. As she brought her knees up to her chest she stared in the direction of the window.

'What a horrible night this is. I have not heard rain like this at all in this realm since I've been here.'

As she pulled the blankets off her body, she climbed out of bed. Her pale feet gently touched the cold floor as she made her way to the open window. She sat in front of the window for a few minutes and allowed the raindrops to kiss her cheek, before closing it and going back to bed.

The following morning La'Sia knocked on Grace's door to awaken her for the school day, but there was no answer. Fearing the worst, she rushed into the room to find an even paler child covered in sweat lying in the bed.

"Grace, Grace….look at you my dear child. You are soaked," replied La'Sia earnestly as she began to take the damp clothes off of Grace. Once she was undressed, she felt her forehead and underneath her chin. 'You are not hot, but you are sweating and you are not cold. My goodness what could have happened to you so quickly?' La'Sia was thinking as she heard a knock at the front door.

La'Sia ran downstairs and opened the door. "Dar, it is you come in, come in," she said quickly. "I need you to take this to Doctor Brawny as fast as you can," she said as she wrote a message quickly on a piece of paper.

"What is wrong, Cona La'Sia?" Dar said.

"Grace is very ill. I believe it is the Goldings disease."

"How did she get that? I thought everyone was immune to that," said Dar quickly.

"You have to remember, Dar, that Grace is not from here, so she does not have immunity. Now go. I do not know how much time we have."

Dar took the note and ran as swiftly as his feet would carry him to Doctor Brawny's office.

When he reached the office a note was posted on the office door:

I will be back in a few hours.

Went to town.

Doc. Zayephious Brawny

Dar yelled angrily and hit the door with his fist before he rushed off to the drawbridge to go to town to get Doc. Brawny.

Back at La'Sia's home, Grace grew much worse. She had proceeded into the second stage of Goldings—hallucinations.

"Grace, Grace….stop screaming. Your mother is not here. She is not dying," La'Sia said as she tried to hold down the raging girl.

"Mom! Mom! Don't die….please don't die. I need you. I need you. Mom! Mom!," Grace yelled while screaming, kicking, and punching.

"Geo help me!" La'Sia called out in desperation.

Grace managed to knock La'Sia to the floor as she ran out the bedroom door and down the stairs. As she was about to hit the front door, Cono Burnos came through the door and caught her.

"Settle down my child, settle down," Cono Burnos said whilst restraining the wild, barely dressed, girl.

He then looked up to see La'Sia rushing down the stairs, "Sia…this child is ill with Goldings."

"Tilo…thank you for catching her. She is so strong. I sent Dar to get Doc Brawny, but he has not returned," she paused when Grace let out a massive scream before falling unconscious.

"Sia, she has gone into stage three of Goldings."

"I know that Tilo. I just got some clothes when she hit stage two. Only two left," she said. "Please bring her upstairs."

"I believe it would be best to keep her down here…if young Dar does not make it back before stage four hits then…"

"You are right," she said cutting him short, "I forgot. Please lay her down on the sofa," she said pointing to a long floral covered chair. "How long do we have?"

"I cannot tell you. Goldings was, or should I say is, different, time-wise, in each person. How on Geo did she get it? All children are supposed to be immune to this disease. How on Geo?" he said slowly looking at Grace.

Dar ran from store to store looking for Doc Brawny when luck finally caught up to him. He saw Doc Brawny coming out of the bakery. He was a chubby old man who wore glasses that constantly slipped off of his nose, and had a short white beard. His head was slightly bald which exposed his bronze skin to the rays of the sun.

"Doc Brawny, Doc Brawny…emergency, emergency," Dar yelled as he ran through the crowd.

"What is the emergency?" Doc Brawny said looking at the panting boy.

"Here. Take this note."

As he read the note he said, "Impossible. No one has Goldings anymore. What stage was she in when you left her?" asked the Doc.

"I don't know….I did not see her."

"Come, we must go quickly. It is a good thing that I am in town, because I have to pick up a few items to help her."

"Please be quick Doc. It took me an hour to find you," replied Dar.

"Sia…look at the girl…it has begun. Stage Four."

"Oh…no….is Doc Brawny going to make it in time?" replied La'Sia while looking at Grace's feet. "Her skin is already turning gold."

La'Sia then fell into Tilo's arms and started to cry, "Oh…Tilo what are we going to do?"

He looked down at the crying woman and no words would enter his mouth. After a few minutes all he could muster to say is, "It is going to be alright. We still have time. We still have time," he said, stroking her brown hair.

"There Dar, we got everything we need," replied Doc. Brawny.

"Are you kidding me? This is what we are going to use," he said looking into the bag.

"Yes it is. Now come on. I believe she is probable in stage three or four right now. We can take Cyan back home."

"Who is Cyan?" Dar said.

Doc Brawny pointed up into the sky, "That is Cyan."

Dar looked up to see a giant bird that looked like it was cut from a jewel. The body and the wings had the appearance of a freshly carved gem, and eyes like emeralds.

"You have a Sapphirest?!"

"I don't have anything. Cyan and I grew up together. He has come for a visit," replied Doc Brawny when Cyan landed. "Hi Cyan… this is Dar. He is a student on campus. He needs a ride back to campus with me. Is that okay?"

Cyan nodded his head. "Well, climb on, boy," replied the Doctor.

Dar looked at the creature with a bit of hesitation. "I know he looks sharp but he is as soft as a pillow. You are not going to cut yourself."

With these comforting words Dar approached the giant bird and climbed up on his back, relieved that Doc Brawny was right.

"Okay Cyan, let's go. I have a sick student to get to."

When the Sapphirest lifted off, Dar nearly fell off his back from the force of the takeoff. Nevertheless when he was in the air, it was the most amazing thing that he had ever experienced.

However, his attention was brought back when they approached campus.

"The girl is at Cona La'Sia's house, Doc," yelled Dar.

"Okay…Cyan, take us down over there," the doctor pointed to the lowly cottage in the corner of campus.

He swooped down so quickly that a part of Dar's breakfast came up and then slid back down his throat. When they landed La'Sia came running outside. "It is up to her neck now, Doctor!"

When he entered the house he said, "Well, well…I never thought the day would come when I would see Goldings reemerging."

He then looked at Dar, "Don't worry we still have quite a bit of time." He subsequently turned to La'Sia and said, "My dear cut this up and start to boil all of it." Doc Brawny handed her a bag of vegetables.

"What is it?"

"The second part of the cure. I must mix together all of the herbs. Too much or too little of either one can be fatal to this young girl."

La'Sia looked into the bag and said, "DOCTOR!!! You are going to use poison tuff, snakeroot clove, and Death Valley rose."

"Yes, I am," he said as he took out his mortar and pestle. "Young man, find me a big tub and fill it with water. Warm water. And when you are done La'Sia, Cona La'Sia, please pour the boiled mixture into the water."

He then looked at Grace, "I am afraid that I misspoke. We do not have much time at all. It is already up to her nose and it has only been ten minutes."

"When did this start?" he turned to La'Sia

"I found her this way at seven o'clock this morning," she said.

"Covered in sweat?"

"Yes, she was."

"And it is only nine o'clock now. I have never seen Goldings this aggressive before. It must have started several hours before she was found, but still to be at four going into stage five," he said seemingly talking to himself.

Dar walked over to Grace and took her hand, "Please don't die Grace. Please don't die."

The doctor quickly came over and smacked her hands out of his. "This is no time to be feeling sorry or mournful. She is not dead yet. If you want her to live get to work. Help that man fill the tub with warm water."

Dar weakly shook his head and got up to assist Cono Burnos. Within ten minutes they managed to fill the tub with water and Cona La'Sia's stew of ingredients was boiling on the stove.

"Ok, I am done grinding up the herbs. Is the pot ready?" the Doc asked.

"Yes it is," she answered.

"Pour it into the tub before the girl is put in. I must rub the herbs over her whole body. Will you help me Cona La'Sia?" he said.

La'Sia kicked Dar and Tilo out of the room while they undressed and rubbed the herbs over Grace's body.

All Dar could do was pace back and forth outside the room until they were allowed back in. Finally he heard a command for him and Cono Burnos to pour the boiling mixture into the tub of water. Within moments of the brew being poured into the tub, Doc Brawny could be seen carrying Grace quickly out of the room.

"Move! Move!....her eyes are starting to open up. When they are completely open we have lost her," he said.

Doc Brawny ran to the tub and dropped Grace into the water. The moment she touched the water steam started to spring forth from her body. Grace became as a marionette doll to the rising steams command, as her back quickly arched out of the tub. The steam rapidly became a golden color as it ascended from her body. Grace's screams could be heard echoing throughout the walls of the house as the mist continued to pour out of her.

Dar could only watch as she was engulfed in this yellowish cloud. He noticed, however, that occasionally small flake-like material was dropping from out the steamy cloud that surrounded her body. When he picked up a piece, he saw that it was a gold flake of Grace's skin stained with blood.

"I did not think it was going to hurt her that badly," Dar managed to say after the ringing of Grace's screams left his ears. As the last remnant of the golden mist left her body, she silently fell back into the tub.

"She was so far along. People I've spoken to who have had Goldings at this stage said that it feels like their very skin is being ripped off – and in a way it is," Doc Brawny said as he too picked up a golden flake. "But all is well now."

"Is this real gold?" Dar asked while opening his palm to the doctor.

"Yes. When the mist cools it drops down in gold flakes," he answered as La'Sia walked slowly by them to the tub. The first thing that she noticed when she looked at Grace in the murky water was that her skin was no longer golden, but returned to its pale creamlike complexion. As she was assessing Grace she noticed that her eyes were beginning to open.

"Grace, Grace, dear how are you feeling?" she asked while waving Dar and Tilo back so as not to see the nude girl.

"It hurts," she muttered before falling unconscious.

"Grace, Grace wake up."

"It is alright, La'Sia. Let her rest now. Take her upstairs and put some clothes on her," Doc Brawny said, looking over the tub at the girl.

"Dar, give me that blanket over there," La'Sia said.

"Good. Stop there while I wrap it around her," she ordered.

When Grace was wrapped in the blanket, Dar came over, picked up Grace's limp body from the water, and carried her upstairs to her room at Cona La'Sia's request.

Placing her on the floor, so as not to get her bed wet, he left the room so that La'Sia could dress her. When he went downstairs, he walked out to the back garden where he wrung out his soaked shirt over the flowers.

Laying his shirt over the stone bench to dry he heard La'Sia calling him into the house. When he went upstairs she motioned for him to place Grace into bed as she was cleaning the water from off the floor.

Slipping his arms under the motionless girl, he placed her gently into her bed and covered her with the blankets. "Can I please stay with her? I promise not to wake her."

Looking up into his pleading eyes she said, "Yes Dar. You may stay."

With no attempt to hide his jubilation he leaped from Grace's bedside and gave Cona La'Sia a hug.

"You're welcome, Dar," she said as she pried him off of her as she finished drying the floor.

When she came downstairs she saw Doc Brawny sitting on the sofa where moments earlier Grace lay dying. "Thank you so much for being here Tilo, but I have to talk to Doc Brawny alone about Grace," she said as she escorted him to the door. Then, a thought occurred to her: "I never asked why you came over today."

"It is not important now," he said smiling.

"It is a lucky thing that you came over today or poor Grace would, would…" she started.

"Well nothing happened, so there is no reason to cry. Good day, and good day to you Doc Brawny," Tilo said.

"Good day," the Doctor answered.

When La'Sia sat down and composed herself, Doc Brawny said, "Why is there a bezoian in the realm of Geo?"

La'Sia nearly lost her voice, "What? What?"

Doc Brawny took off his glasses and cleaned them with a little rag from his pocket. "I can spot a bezoian a mile away," he said putting them back on.

"We don't know. She just appeared here one day," she lied.

"I see," Doc. Brawny said, "Well, she is safe for now from Goldings. The herbs should be flowing through her blood stream as we speak."

"What is the bill, Doctor?"

"For this time…it is nothing, but keep a good eye on her, because Goldings doesn't come from out of nowhere…it is a malicious disease."

"What are you saying?"

"I really don't know. I can't figure out how such and archaic disease could have emerged so quickly. Plus this was the fastest-moving Goldings I have ever encountered. But, no worries, it is all over with."

"Are you sure you don't want any pay?"

"Don't worry about. I got into this field to help people, money means very little to me, but I do have to be on my way. Cyan and I have a lunch date. Good day Cona Gilla," the doctor said as he got up to walk out the door.

"Doctor, you are one of the only people to call me by my last name." She smiled as she watched the doctor fly off on the Sapphirest.

When Doc Brawny left, La'Sia walked upstairs to Grace's room where she heard Dar talking to her. She could hear in his voice that he was distraught.

"Grace....I thought I would lose you today," Dar said as he got on his knees and rested his head over her heart. "I am so sorry." Upon hearing those words La'Sia went downstairs to fix a pot of tea for the long day ahead and to bring him a shirt.

Soon the morning passed into the afternoon, and the afternoon into the evening. Dar only left Grace's side to use the bathroom, then immediately returned to her.

Every now and then La'Sia would bring him some tea and sandwiches to help him keep up his strength. She would smile at him as she watched him look over Grace with such love and concern. She knew that Grace would be in safe hands while Dar watched over her.

As the evening grew long La'Sia entered into the room, "Please don't make me go, Cona La'Sia," Dar said, before she had the chance to speak.

"Dar, it is getting late."

"Please, Cona La'Sia, can I stay?" Dar cried out.

She sighed as she looked into his face again and said, "I will get a place prepared for you."

When she returned she had a pillow and a blanket in hand and said, "After thoughtful consideration you can sleep here on the floor next to Grace. I would offer you a room, but I know you would probably sneak back up here anyway. Good night Dar." She handed him the objects and walked out of the room, slightly closing the door behind her.

Dar spread the blanket out on the floor and lay down. He did not realize how tired he was until his head touched the pillow. As he slept he dreamed of the first time he met Grace.

As the hour grew late, Grace began to stir. She woke up with a slight headache and stomachache.

"I don't feel too good," she whispered while holding her stomach.

She then turned over to step out of bed when she saw Dar's light on the floor. However, she was too ill to care why he was there. She got out of bed and touched him.

"Dar, Dar," she said but he did not wake up. As she made her way to the door she swayed as if she was standing on the deck of a ship in rough seas. When she finally made it down the stairs she rushed out to the back garden as she felt the vomit creeping up her throat, because she knew she would not be able to make it to the bathroom.

After throwing up for what seemed like a lifetime, she felt too weak to go back into the house so she curled up on the stone bench outside. The bench was cool and wet which brought a little comfort to her aching head.

In his dream, Dar heard Grace scream, which woke him up. When he lifted up to see how Grace was doing he saw that she was gone.

Panic rushed through his veins as he ran through the house. He ran downstairs and noticed that the back door was ajar. He quickly darted outside and started to yell her name.

Grace looked over to the side, saw Dar's light, and in a weak soft voice she said "Here I am Dar."

Dar looked over to where the small voice came from. "Grace why are you out here?" he asked as he ran over to her and picked her up.

"I don't feel well, Dar. Put me down," she said as she soon turned to throw up.

"Come on Grace. It is cold out here. Let's get you back inside."

"Can you pick me up again?" she said softly while leaning into his body.

"Sure, come on," he said as he lifted her up and took her back into the house.

He carried her back up the stairs and placed her back into her bed. When she was tucked back in she rolled on her side away from Dar and whispered softly, "I like you Dar Augustus."

Dar paused as a smile creep up on his face. "I like you too Grace Comings."

"I like you very much… I don't want to go back home and be away from you," she softly said as she fell back asleep.

Dar kneeled at her bedside and smiled.

Chapter Fourteen

The Truth is Exposed

The following morning Cona La'Sia came into the room to see Dar kneeling at Grace's bedside asleep. With a little effort she managed to rock him awake.

Dar, groggily, said, "Yes cona."

"How did she do last night?"

"She woke up in the middle of the night and threw up a couple of times."

"Yes, that tends to happen. Did she say anything?"

Dar paused and looked down, "No cona she did not say anything."

Upon those words Grace began to stir. She turned over and opened her eyes. She yawned and stretched her arms.

"Good morning Grace," Cona La'Sia said.

"Good morning Cona La'Sia. Why are you…" and she paused and looked over the side of the bed. "Oh my goodness….Dar's here," she said as she pulled the blankets over her head. "I look horrible. Dar why are you here so early?"

"You don't remember me being here all night long? Remember you got up early this morning," Dar said in a bit of disappointment.

"I don't remember Dar," Grace said with her head still under the blanket, "Can you go downstairs until I get dressed please?"

"Go on downstairs Dar. We will be down shortly," replied Cona La'Sia.

Dar walked out of the room looking back at Grace, "You don't remember," he said softly to himself.

After twenty long minutes Grace and Cona La'Sia came downstairs. Grace came over and gave him a hug and a kiss on the cheek. "Thank you Dar for everything you did for me. You are truly a good friend to me. Cona La'Sia explained everything to me."

In a disappointed voice Dar said, "Friend."

"Yes. Outside of Julia you are my best and dearest friend," said Grace.

With each mention of the word friend Dar felt a nail being driven into his heart. He wanted to hide. He wanted to run. He wanted to scream, but he just repeated in his heart the words she said, 'I like you very much Dar Augustus. I don't want to go back home and be away from you.'

"I am happy you are feeling better Grace. But I have to go. Goodbye," Dar said, and before Grace had a chance to say goodbye he was out the door.

As she watched him walk away she lean against the door post and murmured an "I'm sorry Dar," as she watched his light finally disappear in the distance.

Cona La'Sia stood back and watched Grace in the doorway. But she did not say anything for a few moments.

"Grace…" she finally managed to say.

"Yes, ma'am," she turned her face to the voice.

"I have to go to work. I will be home after school. Stay here and rest for the day," Cona La'Sia said, and she walked out of the house.

She then yelled back, "There is some food on the table for you. Bye Grace."

Grace stood a few minutes in the doorway before she closed the door and sat on the sofa.

When Cona La'Sia reached the school she was greeted by Principal Zarena. "How is she?"

"She is much better, but it was a close one," said Cona La'Sia. "How is her home searching going?"

"Every time Cono Morin thinks he has it, it turns out to be the wrong realm, or time, or wrong time and realm."

"Did Dar come in today?" Cona La'Sia asked.

"Yes he has," she replied.

"I did not think he would. He was up with Grace all night long," Cona La'Sia said.

"Well he is a tough kid," replied Principal Zarena. "Look, he is talking to Eres, Altis, and Leo."

"I don't get kids. They fight one day and are friends another," Cona La'Sia said.

"Here take it," said Dar, giving a bag full of gold dust to Eres.

"You know people with Goldings make the purest gold. It is a shame that they can die if not cured," replied Eres coldly.

"I did not think you had it in you to infect her," said Altis.

"You acted as though I had a choice," said Dar in disgust.

"It is lucky for us that Grace was not immune to the disease," said Leo. "Look at all that gold."

Dar just looked away, refusing to make eye contact with them or the gold he collected when Grace was placed into the tub.

"Go on to class now," Eres said while patting Dar on the head. "We will call you when we need you again. Get now."

Dar walked towards class feeling defeated, as though he would never be freed from the dares of the trio. Stopping to look in his bag for his next period's book, he remembered that he left it in the office. When he went back he saw Cono Burnos talking to Eres in the enclosed courtyard. Curious of their conversation, Dar gently pushed opened the glass door.

Slowly walking into the room, Dar hid behind one of ten massive stone pillars to observe their conversation. However, his attention was briefly taken away as he looked at each pillar in the enclosure.

Every pillar reached ten feet into the air and was as white as the clouds that floated above. Each one had a statue of a great hero on top of it. He only recognized two of them from history class: Sirus the great Ivoro king, and Ula the beautiful sea queen. His focus was quickly brought back when he saw Eres giving Cono Burnos the bag of gold dust. Cono Burnos took the bag and slapped Eres across the face. This was the first time that Dar had ever seen Eres look defeated.

Cono Burnos was still talking to Eres and all Eres was doing was nodding his head up and down in agreement. Eres never looked into Cono Burnos' eyes. When Cono Burnos pointed his finger at a door, Eres immediately started to walk to it.

Dar wanted to stay and observe more, but he did not want to get caught, nor did he want to be late for class, so he ran back into the building. When he reentered the school he let the door slam behind him. When Cono Burnos heard the door shut he traveled to where the sound came from.

"For all of Geo, Cono Burnos and Eres...Eres and Cono Burnos," Dar said over and over again. "I can't believe it, I just can't believe it. Why?"

Dar pondered these thoughts as he entered into Professor Lynos' class.

"Good Morning Dar," Professor Lynos said, "How can I help you?"

Dar just went to his seat without acknowledging Professor Lynos.

"Dar!" he raised his voice.

"Yes, cono. Oh good morning," Dar said.

"Good morning again. How can I help you?" he said again.

"I don't understand what you mean?" Dar said looking at his teacher a bit puzzled.

"It is only first period and I have you second…how can I help you?" Professor Lynos said while pulling up a chair to Dar's desk.

"I am sorry Professor Lynos, I did not realize. I guess I am a bit distracted. I am sorry," Dar said as he stood up to leave.

"There must be a reason why you came here out of all the places," Professor Lynos said while turning around in his seat.

"No reason, Professor Lynos. I just lost track of my mind," Dar replied as he walked out of the classroom door toward his first period teacher's room.

"I see."

Grace could hear the school bell chime that the school day was over. She knew Dar would be at the door shortly, so she walked upstairs to her room and grabbed the brush lying on her night stand. She gently brushed her hair and pulled it back into a ponytail. She then washed her face and went back downstairs to wait for Dar's arrival.

Within moments she could see Dar's light coming over the horizon from the window. She quickly got up and opened the door. Dar could see that she was waving at him from the doorway.

"Hi Dar, how was your day?" she said when he finally arrived.

Out of breath he said, "Good and bad."

"What do you mean good and bad?"

"The good part is seeing you," he paused and looked at her, "but the bad part is….can we go in the house?"

"Sure come in."

Once in the house Dar told Grace all that he had seen with Eres and Cono Burnos.

"What? It can't be true," Grace said.

"But it is. I saw it with my own eyes," replied Dar.

"What do you think this means?"

"I don't know. I will just have to wait and watch and see what comes of it," he said looking at his hands. He then looked up at Grace, "How do you feel?"

"Still a bit ill, but it is not as horrible as it was last night," replied Grace, who soon realized that she had said too much.

"You remember last night," Dar said quickly.

"I....I...." Grace said over and over trying to think of something to say.

Dar took Grace by her shoulders, but she turned her head away from him. "Grace, do you remember last night?" he said.

In a solemn voice she said, "I do."

In rage and joy he said, "Why did you pretend that you did not know I was there?"

Grace could not say anything. "Do you remember what you said to me? Do you Grace!?"

Grace softly said, "I do."

"Then why Grace? Why did you pretend to not remember?" Dar said as his voice cracked from the pain of remembering her lonely word 'friend.'

"I thought it was best for you that I pretended not to remember. I put you into harm's way enough since I have been here. I know it was hard for you to infect me with Goldings and if they knew how I felt…then I fear that things would get much worse."

"You said to me when things first started to happen 'that I do not have the right to make decisions for you,' and likewise you do not have the right to make decisions for me. I care deeply for you Grace Comings. I believe I knew it from the first day that we met."

"How can you care for me Dar?"

"Grace you are the most beautiful and kindhearted girl I have ever met. You are selfless in your deeds and caring of others," replied Dar, taking her hands into his.

Blurting out, she said, "But I am blind."

"And…what does that mean to me?" Dar said.

"I am not pretty enough," she continued as she recalled the cruel words of her aunt.

"You are beautiful."

Grace said nothing else as she heard the gate unlatch, followed by a knock at the door.

"Sia, are you home?" a familiar voice called out.

"It's Cono Burnos, Dar," Grace said.

"I'll go answer the door," replied Dar as he got up and walked slowly over to the door. With every step he took, the floor echoed back with a squeak of warning. When he opened the door he greeted Cono Burnos with a cold hello.

"How are you Dar? Is Cona La'Sia home," he asked.

"No, she has not arrived home from work yet," answered Dar.

"Ooohh….I see. I just came by to see how young Grace was doing."

"I am doing much better, thank you for asking," replied Grace as Dar opened the door wide enough for Cono Burnos to see her.

"Oh….I am so glad to see that you are doing well. But I best be off now. Tell Cona La'Sia I came by," he offered as he tilted the hat on his head and walked away.

The two youths echoed a "good day to you too," as Cono Burnos went through the gate and sauntered down the dusty stone walkway.

"I don't trust him," replied Dar as he shut the door.

"Principal Zarena, Principal Zarena!" yelled Cono Morin as he ran into her office. "I found Grace's home…I found Grace's home!"

"You did Cono Morin? How wonderful!" she said as she walked over to greet Cono Morin.

"But there is one catch," he said.

"Of course…there is always a catch," replied Principal Zarena as she retook her seat. "What is it?"

"Traveling like this is not an exact science so there is a possibility that I will not be able to return her to the same time frame when she left.

"How much would the time disparity be?"

"A few gildiums," he said as he twiddled his fingers.

"How much is a few, Cono?"

"12 or so," he muttered.

Sighing, "Over a year, huh? It is not ideal, but I guess it will do," replied Principal Zarena. "When can she go back?"

"Today, tomorrow, whenever," he replied.

"This is grand news. Please call Cona La'Sia in, will you?" asked Principal Zarena.

Cono Morin walked to the door and in the loudest voice he could gather from his old frame he yelled for Cona La'Sia…who was no more than two feet in front of him.

Cona La'Sia walked over to Cono Morin and rebuked, "Was it necessary to call my name so loud when I was right here? Put on your glasses, Cono Morin."

"Yes, Principal Zarena," she then said as she walked into the office.

"I have grand news for you," she paused as she looked at the slender lady. "Cono Morin has found Grace's home."

"Really. Oh…Oh…that is great," she said softly as she reached up to twirl a lose strand of brown hair with her finger.

"Why do you sound so sad, Cona La'Sia? Earlier you were ready for her to go home."

"Well, I have become so attached to that little girl," replied Cona La'Sia.

"You knew that she was not going to be staying here for long," replied the principal.

"I know, I know…and I am truly happy for her because it is not safe here for her, but I cannot help myself from feeling this way. I have grown to really love her." She hesitated. "I'll tell her the good news when I go home," she said as she walked out of the office.

Principal Zarena yelled after her, "She will be going home tomorrow!…Cona La'Sia!"

Cono Morin looked at Cona La'Sia, and then at the folded piece of paper in his hand, and said, "I wish I did not find out where she lived after all, but, oh well, back to the lab."

Chapter Fifteen

Going Home

Time passed so quickly and before she knew it Cona La'Sia found herself standing several steps from her own door. She stared at the weathered wooden door with its fading paint and sighed with every step that she took across the pebbled pathway toward that door. She found herself holding on to the door knob fearing to turn it. She bowed her head and said softly, "This is the only time that I have ever regretted coming home."

As she pushed open the door she found Grace and Dar talking in the living room. She greeted the youths with a kind hello that was draped in sadness.

"What is the matter?" inquired Grace.

"Oh…nothing just tired," she said.

Dar knew she was lying as he gazed into her redden eyes, but he dare not say anything so as to not alarm Grace.

"Do you want to go on a walk? You've been in this house all day…I know you could use some fresh air," Dar said as he took Grace's hand.

"You don't have to do that," replied Cona La'Sia as her voice cracked. "Have a seat you two. I have some good news. Cono Morin has found Grace's home and she will be leaving us tomorrow."

"What!" Grace said as she jumped to her feet. She looked at Dar and then towards Cona La'Sia and said, "That is not good news. Why tomorrow? Why not the next day? Did anyone ask me when I wanted to leave? No, they did not. This is so unfair!" she said in exasperation as she sat down.

"I know Grace, but it is what it is," she said. "You knew when you came here that it would not be forever."

"I know," Grace said softly as the room soon drained of any more words. The only audible sounds were the soft sobs rising from Cona La'Sia who tried to muffle them by covering her mouth.

"This is very unfair," Grace murmured.

Cona La'Sia looked up at the angry girl and said, "Tomorrow, you will be dressed in the clothes that you came here with and Principal Zarena will allow Dar to go with you to make sure you get home safe. Cono Morin will travel with you back to your time."

Dar looked up at Cona La'Sia, "I can go?"

"Only as a guide and a protector to her," replied Cona La'Sia, "but you must return with Cono Morin."

In a soft voice Grace said, "You know what Dar? I think that walk might just be a good idea…let's go."

Dar looked at Cona La'Sia who silently mouthed 'go' as she wiped the tears that started to run down her face.

Grace grabbed the rod Dar had made for her and started towards the door with Dar trailing behind.

When they left the front gate Grace turned to Dar, wrapped her arms around him, and said "I want to go home, but I don't want to go home. I don't know what to do."

"You have to go home Grace…that is the right choice," replied Dar.

"But…" she said as Dar cut her off.

"I know what you are going to say, but don't say it Grace," said Dar. "It is going to be hard enough to say goodbye as it is. And since we only have this day to say our goodbyes…let's go say goodbye to Ren, Aphreneea, and Mikos."

Grace nodded her head as she allowed Dar to take the lead. As they walked down the pebbled path to the stone-paved path of the school campus, Grace thought of all the wonderful times she had there. She thought about the day they went to Ice Lake and the great times she had with Aphreneea and Ren. Soon these thoughts overwhelmed her and she could no longer hold back her tears.

She dropped to her knees and sobbed so loudly that the heavens echoed her pain and it began to rain and thunder. Dar tried to pick her up, but she refused to move and pushed him away, causing him to lose his balance. When he got up he slowly walked over to her and placed his arms around her shoulders. He created a stone shelter above them as the rain became heavier.

"Why… Why do I have to leave now?" she said looking up at Dar, realizing what she was now losing.

"I'm going to miss you too, Grace," he said as he held her hand to his heart. "It looks like the rain has slowed down a little. Let's go on to Aphreneea and Ren's" he said, lowering the shelter.

"No. Do we have to, Dar? Can't we stay here for a little longer?"

"Sure," he said as he sat back down beside her on the wet stone pavement. He would occasionally look down at her leaning on his shoulder, but he dared not to speak. Neither one wanted to utter a word in hope that this situation was a bad dream, a nightmare that they would awake from and laugh about later.

But their dream was soon broken when Aphreneea came by. "What are you two doing sitting on this wet ground?" she said as she looked at them through her emerald eyes.

"Get up," she said pulling Grace off of the ground. "You are soaked and wet and covered in gravel. Come on let's go," she said as she started to walk towards her dormitory with Grace in tow.

"Where are we going?" Grace said trailing behind Aphreneea.

"To get you some dry clothing," she said. "You look a mess — and your hair looks horrible."

Dar got up from the ground and looked at the two girls walking down the pavement to the girl's dormitory. He wanted to follow but something inside of him caused him to linger. Every time he tried to move he was frozen in place.

When they finally reached the dormitory, Aphreneea immediately instructed Grace to change into some dry clothes she placed in her hands. When Grace was finished she sat her down on the floor and started to comb her hair.

"Now tell me, what is the matter?" Aphreneea said in a sympathetic tone of voice that Grace had never heard from her before. Normally she had a hard but kind voice – never sympathetic.

"I have to go home tomorrow," she said.

"And what is wrong with that?" she said as she continued to comb her hair.

"I told Dar that I liked him."

"About time, but you don't live so far away that he will not be able to reach you," she said as she began to braid her hair.

"I do live far away – further than you realize, Aphreneea. When I go home I will never see him again. I did not think anyone would ever like an ugly blind girl. But he does. He told me," Grace said as she turned around to face her.

"Turn back around I am not done yet. First thing, you are not ugly – who in the world gives the criteria for who is beautiful and who is ugly?" Aphreneea questioned.

"I don't know. I don't look like everyone else," she said.

"And that is what makes you you. You can't even see yourself, so how do you know that you are not beautiful?" Aphreneea asked.

"I don't know. My aunt always called me ugly," she said.

"You cannot go off the words of others to determine who you are. You must determine that for yourself," Aphreneea concluded as she finished her braid. "Dar should be here shortly to come and get you."

"Actually we were coming over here to see you and Ren," she said.

"Ren, well," Aphreneea was saying as she came into the room. "Well speak of the detan, I guess she is here."

"Good. I came here to tell you two goodbye. I am going home tomorrow."

"We are going to miss you, Grace. How long will it take you to go back to Stone Falls?" inquired Aphreneea, but was interrupted by a knock at the door.

"Well, it is you Dar. It took long enough for you to get here," she said when she opened the door. "Now, what was I saying? Oh, I remember. How long will it take you to go back to Stone Falls?"

"A few days," replied Dar.

"Dar, as I said when I first met Grace, let her answer for herself." She turned to Grace, "I will miss you, Grace."

"Me too," Ren said, wrapping her arms around Grace's waist, crying.

"Ren," replied Aphreneea.

"Where can we find Mikos?" asked Dar.

"I don't know…why are you asking me?" said Aphreneea feistily.

"I thought, because you…"

"Mikos and I are taking some time away from one another," she interjected.

"If you want to find that forgetful boy…look in his room."

"Thank you," Grace said as she pried Ren's arms from around her waist. "I will miss you two," she said as she gave them each a hug.

She then turned to Aphreneea and said, "Thank you so much for talking with me, Aphreneea."

"No problem. I will bring your clothes over to Cona La'Sia's house when they are clean," she said as she waved bye to them.

As they closed Ren and Aphreneea's dorm room door Grace said, "What took you so long?"

"I really don't know. I just couldn't make myself move," he said.

"Oooohh, I see. I am sure going to miss this place. Walking down the stone pathways and smelling the sweet scents that only belong to Geo," she said.

"Don't talk about it as though you are gone yet. Enjoy every moment that you are here," he said walking up to the boy's dormitory stairs.

"Mikos's room is three doors down to the right," she said as she entered the hallways of the dormitory.

"Yes it is," he replied.

"Should I or you break the news?" she questioned.

"I think you will do a better job," he replied with a smile on his face as they reached his door.

Grace gently knocked on the door until Mikos opened it. "Oh....come in. I did not know you two were coming over. Come in, come in, have a seat. Would you like a cup of Jasper

Juice?" he offered a bit frazzled as he led them into the small dormitory room.

"I thought you did not like Jasper Juice, Mikos," said Grace.

"I guess the slug-skunk taste has grown on me."

"Well, I guess I am happy to hear that," she said.

"What brings you over this way?"

"I just came to say goodbye. I am going home tomorrow."

"Why so suddenly?"

"It's just time."

"I am going to miss you Grace," he said as he got up and gave her a hug.

"I am going to miss you too, Mikos," replied Grace as a question came to her.

"Mikos, before I go. What did you forget to do or give Aphreneea?" asked Grace.

"I don't want to talk about it," he replied.

"I understand. Have a good..." started Grace.

"I forgot about our Mir," replied Mikos.

"Mir," she said.

"Mir is when you set up a time to meet with one another for a festive occasion," Dar said.

"You didn't," she said.

"I did," he replied, "and she was so upset."

"What did you say?" she asked.

"I told her the truth…that I forgot," he simply replied.

"Mikos, Mikos, Mikos," she said, "I don't have all the answers in the world, but is there something she really wants that you can give her as a forgive-me gift?"

"She did not say anything," he answered.

"Is there something special that you two did together and is special to you two? When you think of that thing…turn that into a gift."

"Can you give an example?" he said.

"A chunk of ice from that lake place…something like that," she said.

"That sounds like a good idea. I will think about something," he said as he looked out the window lost in his thoughts.

Dar leaned over to Grace while Mikos was thinking of the perfect gift and whispered, "We have to go. It is getting late."

He then spoke up and said, "It is getting late Mikos and she still has to pack."

"Will you come back to visit us one day?" asked Mikos as he stood up and walked them to his doorway to see them off.

"I really don't know Mikos. Luck brought me here, maybe it will bring me back," she said.

As they walked outside into the warmth of the stormy weather she said, "You know what Dar? I am really going to miss this place. I laughed so much here. I learned things that I would have never learned at home and I gained three good friends." She turned to him. "How can I give it all up and just forget?"

"Then don't forget. Remember us. Think of us. For I know I will always be thinking of you," he declared.

Grace intertwined her arm in his, leaned her head on his shoulder, and said softly, "I wish we had more time together. We truly only had one day."

"That is not right. We had many days together. Remember our trip to the Ice lake and every day that we would sit together." He turned to her. "We had many gildiums together." All she could do was smile at this boy who she would never see beyond his beautiful white spherical light.

"So, what do you want to do tonight…since this is our last night together?"

In a solemn voice he said, "To say our goodbyes."

"What?! This is our last night together and you want to say goodbye? Don't you want to spend time with me…with the one you said you cared for?" she said with a broken heart.

"I did not mean it that way," he defended. "When people say goodbye to someone they may never see again, they never get the chance to say it twice. It is usually that one time in that one moment. So many times I wished I had the chance to say a second goodbye to someone I really cared for, and I want the chance to say a second goodbye to you."

"Dar, that is very profound." She leaned over, gave him a kiss on the cheek, and whispered, "Goodbye Dar."

Dar then turned and pulled her closer as he cupped her face in his hand. As he looked into those all familiar ice blue eyes he ran two fingers down her lips. Sensing that this was maybe the last chance for him to express his feelings he leaned in and lightly kissed her several times on the lips – holding the last one.

Slowly Grace wrapped her arms around his neck. It was not until this moment that she truly understood what was written in Julia's romance novels.

Dar slowly pulled away and she asked breathlessly, "Aren't you going to say good-bye?"

Dar shook his head and whispered, "I can't."

"Then I will wait," she said as she sunk into his arms for a few more moments.

They started their walk back to the house, talking about all the things they did together and the things they learned.

"No one will ever believe me about the Elementer's history or the fire mountain story," she replied.

"Maybe you can become a writer," he replied.

"Dar, a blind person cannot become a writer," she replied.

"Yes they can. If you can talk then you can become a writer. Talk it out and have someone write it down."

"You are a genius," she replied.

"I know," he said with a smile.

"And you are boastful," she said with a giggle.

"I am not. I just know the truth."

"Okay…I guess I will say goodnight."

"Why do you say that?"

"We are back home. I can smell Cona La'Sia's flower of the month," she said.

"I am going to miss that nose of yours," he said as he touched the tip of it. "Goodnight Grace."

"Aren't you going to walk me to the door?" she questioned as she placed her hand on the fence.

"I…I…can't. I'll see you tomorrow," he said.

"Goodnight, Dar."

"Goodnight, Grace."

The next day rolled around in what seemed to be minutes. Cona La'Sia had Grace's old clothing laid out on her bed. Picking up her dress and shoes she said. "Well, these are really familiar. I missed these old things."

"You know you do not have to leave so early. You can stay for lunch or even dinner," said Cona La'Sia, wiping away some tears.

"It is best that I leave early. The longer I stay, the harder it will be for me to leave," she replied. She then looked up at Cona La'Sia and said, "My mom died a long time ago and I miss her very much. Every single day after her death I wanted her back. But since I've been here I haven't had those feelings. And I just wanted to say thank you." Grace ended as she gave her a hug.

"I will not forget you, Grace Comings," she replied when a knock came at the front door. Cona La'Sia held her for a few more seconds and then went downstairs to answer the door.

"Cono Burnos…what are you doing here?" she said as she opened the door to the jet black haired individual.

"I came to say farewell to Grace," he replied.

"How kind of you," she said, "come in. Grace! There is some- one here for you."

Thinking that it was Dar coming to get her she rushed downstairs to find no light at all. "Who is it Cona La'Sia?"

"It is Cono Burnos coming to see you off," she said with a smile in her voice.

"Oh…thank you Cono Burnos. I am excited about going home. It has been so long."

"Really? And where do you live again?" he questioned the young girl.

"Stone Falls," she replied quickly.

"I see. I have a relative who lives there. Maybe I will come visit you sometime," he said before adding, "I see that the clothing of that region has really changed since I have been there."

"Will you have a cup of tea?" Cona La'Sia quickly interjected.

"No, thank you Sia, I just came by to say goodbye to Grace."

"Okay, well you have a nice day, Tilo," she said as she walked him to the door.

When the door shut, Grace said, "What if he comes to visit and no one knows who I am?"

"To tell you the honest truth Grace, I believe Tilo knows you are not from this realm. He made note of that by commenting on your clothing."

"Why did he not just say so?"

"I guess he was trying to have some discretion, because you as a bezoian shouldn't be here."

"I see…When will Cono Morin be here?"

"He should be here shortly. I saw him coming down the road," Cona La'Sia said when a knock came at the door. When she opened it, standing in the doorway was old Cono Morin in a ridiculous outfit. Dumbstruck, Cona La'Sia examined him, starting with the black hat on his head, and moving to the shiny green shoes on his feet, then going back to the purple and blue checkered vest and jacket he had on with black pants that flared at the bottom.

"Cono Morin, why are you dressed like that, and with no shirt on?" Cona La'Sia said in horror.

"Well, Cona La'Sia, I studied up on the fashion of that era and I want to fit in for the few moments I am going to be there," he replied while cuffing his hands in his jacket folds.

"Cono Morin, I believe you have studied up on the wrong era. Look at Grace's clothes and look at yours. Do you think that men dress like that….if she is dressed like this?"

"Maybe, but I will find out won't I?" he said smugly.

"Not at the risk of leaving her in the wrong time?"

"I assure you that I have found the right time and place," he said holding up a worn missing person sign with Grace's face on it, "I found this in a wooden area nailed to a tree outside of a little town."

Taking the flyer out of his hands she said nicely, "You are just excited to be traveling…without limits. Did you go into the town?

"No…I was not dress appropriately yet. I only saw a couple of young boys around Dar's age - not mature men like myself," he said placing his hands back into the folds of his jacket as he rocked back and forth on his heels.

"I believe you still missed the mark with that outfit."

Stopping his motion, "Well…we will see won't we."

"You will see…"

"Do I need anything?" Grace interjected as she sensed that they might have forgotten she was there.

Looking at the young girl facing them, La'Sia motioned for a dresser drawer where she took out a small box. "I know that they said you could not take anything from this realm, but I want you to have this," she said as she pulled a necklace from the box.

"It feels beautiful, Cona La'Sia. What does it look like?" she asked.

"It is a circle of small roses cut from laplazuli stone…laplazuli is the color of the sea."

"Thank you Cona La'Sia," Grace said as she gave her a big hug.

Spotting the small cottage in the distance Dar prepared himself for his final time with Grace. Shaking off the nerves he rehearsed a few phrases he came up with, until he was interrupted when he came face to face with Cono Burnos.

"Good morning to you Dar," he said.

"Good morning Cono Burnos."

"It is a beautiful day to travel, isn't it?" he said looking towards the sky.

"Yes it is, cono."

"You want to hear a secret? A good Traveler knows not to travel in a thunderstorm. It disrupts the rip," he replied.

"Why is that relevant to us, cono?"

"I always thought that fact was interesting, and I usually like to share it when given the chance."

"Then it is not much of a secret is it," replied Dar.

Cono Burnos laughed and said, "I guess it is not."

"Well, thank all of Geo for a clear blue sky today," Dar said while looking towards Cona La'Sia's house.

"Well, I don't want to keep you. I know you are anxious to see sweet Grace off. Good day," he said, walking down the stone walkway towards the campus while Dar continued toward the little cottage tucked in the corner.

At the moment of his arrival Cono Morin said, "It is time to go. You have finally arrived."

"Well Dar, look at you in those clothes. It seems as though someone may have gotten it right," Cona La'Sia said, looking at him in his brown pants with his brown suspenders and white button-up shirt.

"I feel and I look stupid," was all Dar could manage to say as he looked at the clothing Professor Morin brought to him earlier.

"I bet you look dashing," Grace said.

"Okay, okay, kids let's go so I can come back and get some more work done," Cono Morin said.

"Are we going to go back to the Whispering Woods to get back to my home?" asked Grace.

"No, we are going to go in the front yard and take you back home," Cono Morin said.

"Come on, let's go," he said as he guided Grace and Dar to the front yard. "Stay in the house Cona La'Sia, you do not want to be caught in the residue."

Cono Morin stepped a little away from the two youths toward an open area, and stretched forth his hands and arms. His hands started to glow red hot like they were being heated by a furnace. He raised his hands, then brought them down with a swipe, and parted what can only be described as time and space.

"Come on kids, let's go. This portal will not stay open for too long."

Dar grabbed Grace's hand and proceeded towards the whirling black rip. The moment they were in the mist of the portal a lightning bolt came and struck the portal, closing the rip behind them. The force of the impact caused Cono Morin to fly back into Cona La'Sia's arms. Cona La'Sia pushed Cono Morin off of her and cried Grace's name at the top of her lungs.

"Hang on to me Grace!" Dar yelled.

"Don't let me go!" she bellowed as they were pushed and pulled through the whirling space of the rip.

"Wrap your legs around my waist if you can," he said to Grace who immediately found her way to his body.

In the mist of the swirling blackness of the rip, Dar could see pockets of light emerge and disappear. When he saw another pocket of light emerge, he quickly shifted his and Grace's bodies toward the opening. As they drew closer to the light the force of the pull was so strong that Grace could not hold on to Dar, who too was sucked through the pocket of light.

"Grace, Grace…stop crying we are out of the rip," he said while lying on his back, deeply breathing.

In a panic stricken voice she said, "Where are we?"

He slowly sat up, looked around, and said, "I'm home."

"Cono Morin where are the kids? Where are they!?" Cona La'Sia yelled, shaking him until his glasses fell off his face.

"I don't know. But I can find them. I will have to follow my own residue," he said. "Let me go, Cona La'Sia, before it disappears and they are lost forever." When she did, he created a rip and jumped through after the lost children.

"What do you mean 'I'm home'?" Grace said.

"I'm home Grace," he said with shock and laughter. "I have not been home since my parents died." He paused and looked up at the blue sky. "It still smells the same. Nothing has changed at all about this place."

He then looked down a narrow dirt road. "My house is right down that road over that small hill. My mother would be hanging clothes or cooking at this time. Sometimes she would be doing both. She was the best at whatever she did."

"Would you like to go visit you home?" questioned Grace.

"Cono Morin will come looking for us…if we are not here he may leave."

"I understand."

"But I really would like to see my home again. Take off that necklace and I will leave it on top of my jacket, so that he knows we came here. We won't be gone long, it is all probably in ruins. It has been eight years."

"The one thing that I have learned is that memories, no matter how long it has been, don't change much. Even if your house is in ruins, you will remember it for what it was. But the true question is can you handle seeing your home again after so long?"

"I can," he said as he got off the ground.

As they began their journey toward his home Dar told Grace of all the fun things he and his parents use to do in the woods. However, he abruptly ended his story when he noticed smoke rising from the chimney of his home. "Someone has moved into my old home," he said.

"Well, it has been a long time. Maybe a beggar or a traveler has stopped in to rest," she answered.

"No, it is not that. It is clean, it is familiar," he replied, "I remember this."

As they approached closer, they could smell the sweet scent of stew cooking on the stove and a woman humming a tune, hanging clothing on a line.

"It can't be," Dar said softly as he approached the cottage and the woman closer. "Mother."

The woman turned around and looked up to have her fiery burnt orange eyes meet that of Dar's. As they stared at one another the wind danced around them, causing her long blond hair to blow across her face and her ankle length blue dress to move across her body. She dropped her clothes on the ground and slowly approached Dar gently touching his face and said, "My son?" Grace could hear Dar's sobs resonating in his throat.

"Yes, it is me, mother," Dar said releasing Grace's hand and wrapping his arms around his mother. Grace could feel that the woman was looking at her as she embraced Dar.

"Come. We should go inside," she said leading them to the cottage.

Dar looked at the small cottage with its thatched roofing and little chimney emerging from the center. He looked at the two diamond shaped windows nestled on both sides of the wooden doorway with plants hung on them. The color of the house was just as he remembered it to be, a pale egg yolk color – he hated it.

Arriving inside, she sat them down on the sofa while she got two cups of water. "You two must be tired," she called from the kitchen.

When she came back she handed them each a cup of water and said, "Dar look at you. You are so handsome."

"Aren't you shocked to see me?" he asked. "How did you know it was me?"

"My boy, I am very shocked to see you. I said goodbye to my eight year old son this morning and I turn around to see a fifteen, sixteen year old son in front of me," she answered calmly while sipping her tea. "And Dar, I know my son's face anywhere, no matter how old you have gotten. Tell me, how did you two get here?"

"I was taking Grace back home to her time when we were separated from our Traveler," he replied.

The woman looked at the little girl and said, "Hello dear, my name is Aurora Augustus."

"My name is Grace Comings, ma'am. It is very nice to meet you."

"No, the pleasure is all mine. It is a treat when a mother could see how her son will look years from now. You remind me of your father Dar," she replied with a smile until she noticed that Dar dropped his head. "Oh….I guess this is more of a treat then I really realized it to be."

She then came over and sat next to him and said, "It is alright Dar."

Without noticing what he was saying, he fell into his mother's bosom and cried, "No, it's not. The reason you and father died was because of me. It is all my fault. If I had listened, if I only had listened to you, you would still be alive. You died to protect me. You told me to stay home and I didn't and…and…and you died to protect me. I am so sorry, I am so sorry. Do you forgive me?"

"Ohhhh….Dar. For a parent to sacrifice their life for their child's is a great honor. It is not your fault and there is nothing to forgive. I would die for you a million times over because you are my son."

"But you would have lived if I had only listened," he sobbed.

"Are you positive that I would have lived?" she questioned.

"What?" he said as he paused to consider what she just said. "You probably would have. You and dad were fighting so hard," he finally answered.

"You did not answer my question Dar. Are you positive that we would have lived?"

"No, I am not," he said taken back by his own words.

"That is what I want you to remember. Life is a maze of probabilities. You were so certain that we were going to live that you did not take into consideration that we were meant to die."

Dar was stunned into silence. "My only regret about dying is that you were there to see it, not the dying part. I will miss you, Dar. But I am so happy that I got the chance to see you all grown up."

"Where is dad?"

"He took you out hunting," she replied.

"What!? What was he wearing today?" His mother described the outfit his father had on and the outfit she put on him.

"Today is the day!" he exclaimed as he rushed towards the door.

"Sit down Dar," his mother demanded.

"But we have to go out and save father, before it is too late," he pleaded with her.

"No, we will not," she ordered. "You cannot alter the future. You can only delay the inevitable."

"What do you mean?" he said.

"If you save us today then we may die tomorrow. If you save us tomorrow we may die two days from now. Our death is written in the cosmos. It cannot be altered."

Angrily he said, "So you are saying that I have to sit by and watch you two die again!"

"I am saying that you will sit back and let things flow as they should."

"I can't let that happen. I will not see you two die again."

In a kind, motherly tone she said as she whirled her hands in a circle, "You were a stubborn boy."

Dar suddenly found himself encased in an air bubble that was as strong as steel.

"Let me out mother!" he yelled while tears welled up in his eyes. "I don't want you to die again. Please! Please!" he begged as he pounded on the floating cell. "Don't do this to me."

"That is not your choice Dar, and this is a lesson that you truly must learn," she said.

"Please! Please! Mother. Please!!" he said over and over again.

She then moved towards the floating jail and started to push it into the back room. "What are you doing?" he cried.

"You told me that I told you to stay home. I cannot allow him to see himself," she said to him. She then turned to Grace and said, "Follow me!"

She nodded her head and with outstretched hands felt her way towards Dar's light.

"Hmmm," Aurora sounded as she watched the young girl slowly maneuver towards her son, "You can see him can't you?"

Her comment nearly knocked Grace off her feet. "How, how do you know that?" she asked when Aurora took her by the hand.

"Only a theory. I noticed it when you two first arrived, but I believe…" Before she could finish her statement young Dar came into the house screaming. "Quickly, get in here," she said as she closed the door behind them.

Grace could hear that the son was saying something to his mother when she heard the door shut. "It's all over," Dar murmured. "They are going to die and here I am stuck in this stupid bubble," he said as he kicked the invisible shield.

Grace came over and touched the bubble, "At least you got to say your second goodbye," she said as she knelt down and sat next to the bubble.

Dar understood that Grace was trying to comfort him, but he did not want to hear anything about a second goodbye. After about ten minutes she heard the front door open and shut again.

"There I go," Dar said with his head in his knees, "I should be out of here shortly."

"What do you mean?" questioned Grace.

"With a structure like this …when an Elementer dies so does this, in a way," he said.

Grace just looked up at Dar who never lifted his head from his knees. After about fifteen minutes she heard him drop to the ground.

"I'll be back, Grace," he said as he bolted out of the house.

He ran with all of his might to the battlefield. By the time he arrived it was too late. His parents lay slain on the ground, and he himself was passed out on top of them.

'I don't remember passing out,' he said to himself as he walked over to the bodies. He went over, picked himself up from his parents, and started to walk back to the house when he saw someone in the shadows. He then camouflaged himself and his younger self with leaves. He was only two feet away from his parents when the shadowy feature emerged.

To his shock and amazement it was Cono Burnos. He was slightly younger and had shorter hair, but there was no mistaking who it was. He came over, knelt down over their bodies, and spit on them.

When Dar saw this he burned with rage. At that moment he wanted to kill Cono Burnos. The only thing holding him back was the sleeping boy in his arms.

"What a waste of time," he replied as he stood up and walked away.

When he was gone, Dar emerged from hiding, walked back over to his parents, said his goodbyes, and went slowly back to the house leaving a trail of tears behind him.

Back at the house he was greeted by Grace. "I now know how I made it back to the house that day," he explained as he laid the sleeping boy on the chair. "We should go back to where we originally arrived. I can't let myself see himself."

"I understand," she said as they got up and walked out of the house. When they were on the top of the hill they could hear the little boy yelling for his parents before the sound of his words were silenced by his own sobs. Grace grabbed Dar by his hands and pulled him as close as she could while still walking. She knew at this time that saying nothing was the best comfort there was.

When they came back to where they originally fell through the rip, Dar saw Cono Morin waiting for them. "There you two are. I was sure that this was the spot because this is where the trail of you two ends." He looked up and down at Dar's clothing and said, "You look a mess. Let's get you back home. You can't take Grace home looking like that now, can you?" Dar did not say a word as he picked up the jacket and the necklace they left behind. Grace did not say a word as she felt Dar putting the necklace back on her. Cono Morin opened a rip and all three of them walked through, back to Geo.

When they arrived back at Cona La'Sia's home Principal Zarena was waiting there for them. After he changed his clothing from the blood-covered mess, he described all that happened to them, with the exception of Cono Burnos. Bitterness had settled in his heart and he wanted revenge. He did not want anyone to exact punishment on Burnos but him.

As Grace watched him tell the story she noticed that his light was beginning to change a crimson color. However, by the end of his story his light started to slowly fade back into the pure white light that she was more familiar with.

"I think I will go home and lay down. If you don't mind, can we take Grace back tomorrow?" asked Dar.

"No one is traveling anywhere," said Principal Zarena. "It is not safe. Are you sure there is no one who wishes you harm?" she questioned Dar.

"No one."

Grace just looked at Dar's now pinkish light, and thought to herself 'something is terribly wrong.'

"May I go, cona?" asked Dar again.

"No, it is not safe for you to go back to your dormitory."

Dar let out a deep sigh of frustration as he walked around to the back of the house.

"He is not pleased," said Cona La'Sia.

"At this point I am not worried about how he feels. I sense that there is more to this story then he is letting on. I cannot take the chance of his stubbornness endangering those students living in the dormitory," the principal concluded.

"You are right," said Cona La'Sia, watching Grace follow Dar.

"Where are you going?" Grace asked when she caught up to him.

"Home."

"Why don't you stay here where it is safe?"

"Do you really think it is safe anywhere?"

"It is safer here in the company of many."

"Did this company stop us from flying through a rip? No, it did not."

"We are well prepared now and even better so if you tell them the truth."

"The truth is pointless."

"Dar, what is the matter with you? Why are you still protecting those boys? Haven't they done enough to you?" Grace said in a quiet rebuke, then stopped when she sensed she was getting loud.

"I could care less about Altis, Eres, and Leo right now," Dar said in a bitter voice that shocked Grace. "Just leave me alone, Grace," he said coldly as he moved towards the back fence. "Go back around front."

"I will not. Stop pushing people away when you need them the most. I am here."

"What do you want from me? What do you want me to say? That I could not once again save them from dying? That once again I failed my parents. That once again I was there when they died and could do NOTHING. What Grace? What can you say to relieve this for me?"

Silenced by his words, she only watched as he made his way through the back gate towards campus.

Dar knew all too well how to maneuver through the back hedges of Cona La'Sia's home because of the numerous times he visited Grace. As he jumped over familiar bushes and ducked under hanging tree branches he allowed his mind to race. His trance was only broken when he heard someone behind him.

Stopping, he turned to find Grace. "Didn't I say…" but he was hushed by her.

"You asked me a question, but you never gave me a chance to answer. You said 'what can you say to relieve my pain?' It took me a few moments to think of the right words to say and how to say it. The funny thing is…I could not think of anything but this," she said as she came up to him and gave him a hug. "My friend Julia would always give me a hug when I would miss my mother. She would always say to just pretend for a moment that she was her and it would be like giving her a hug."

Sighing, he quietly embraced her and then whispered as if speaking to his mother, "I saw who took you away from me. I saw Cono Burnos. He is the reason you are dead.

Upon hearing his words Grace said, "Cono Burnos."

"Yes, he is the reason that my parents are dead. I saw him spit on their bodies."

"But their death did not exact the results that I wanted," a voice called out.

"Where are you?" Dar demanded as he released Grace.

"Look up, son of Dious," the voice said.

"You killed my parents!" Dar yelled at him as he positioned Grace behind him.

"Ah, I thought I saw someone that day, but who would have guessed that it was you. But you have something wrong: I did not kill your parents. From what I recall a particular beast killed your parents," he replied.

"One that you probably brought back to our realm," he retorted.

"Maybe so, maybe so" he said smugly, "but you cannot change the past now, can you? Aurora knew that all too well."

"What do you mean by that?" questioned Dar.

"Well, you really would like to know, wouldn't you? Maybe another day," he said as he fell into a rip.

"Dar," Grace said softly behind him, "We must tell them."

Dar nodded as the gravity of the situation was coming to light. As they started their walk back through the hedges to Cona La'Sia's house Dar looked up and watched the sun beams dance through the tree canopy as his mind was blanketed with the image of Cono Burnos standing over his parents.

Upon their arrival back at Cona La'Sia's home, Dar gathered together the adults and started telling them about all of the dares the trio had made him do. He told them why Grace was on Fire Mountain, and he told them the whole story of what he saw when he went back into the past.

"Why did you wait so long to tell us?" said Principal Zarena.

"I don't know. It was no big deal in the beginning, but then it started to get worst," he said.

"And Grace, you knew about this, and you allowed yourself to get infected with Goldings?" said Cona La'Sia, heartbroken. "How could you?"

"She did it for me, Cona La'Sia, don't be mad at her," Dar said.

"And you! You were willing to sacrifice her life to keep a dare, a stupid dare," she chastised him.

"I did not realize it would go that far."

"You didn't realize! How could you not know?" she said as she slowly approached him, before the principal intercepted her.

"You will be staying here tonight under the protection of Professor Lynos, Dar." The principal then turned to Morin and said, "Quickly, go get Professor Lynos for me."

"I've been traveling a lot lately," he said, "And I even get to travel to the campus. A very short distance without getting into trouble," he said sarcastically.

"Cono Morin, if you do not leave at this moment you…," she paused at which point he jumped through a rip.

Within seconds Cono Morin was in Professor Lynos' room describing the situation to him.

"Finally, that boy has spoken up."

"You knew about it, Lynos," Cono Morin said.

"I knew something like that was going on, but I did not know that it was so bad," he replied.

"Principal Zarena needs you to be their guardian tonight."

"It would be my honor. Dious and Aurora were very good people," Professor Lynos said, "Let's go."

Cono Morin guided Professor Lynos through a rip back to Cona La'Sia's home, and found it on fire. "What happened?" Professor Lynos exclaimed.

"They attacked us so quickly," Principal Zarena said. "I did not know they were going to move so swiftly. I thought we had more time."

"Who attacked?" he questioned.

"Altis, Eres, Leo, and Cono Burnos at the lead," said Cona La'Sia rubbing the blood from her head.

"Did they take both of the children?" Professor Lynos asked as he created a rain cloud over the house to put out the fire.

"Yes, they did," Principal Zarena replied.

"Why did they take Dar? I thought they were only after Grace, or maybe it was never Grace that they were truly after…" he said.

"What do you mean?" questioned Cona La'Sia.

"Those boys were making Dar do dares long before Grace came into the picture. What if they were after Dar the whole time…like a test…a training exercise."

"You knew about these dares professor and you did nothing," the principal interjected.

"They were small things, nothing too big or too dangerous. However, they just increased the dares to a higher extent when she came."

"And still you stayed silent? Nevertheless, training him for what?" Principal Zarena asked.

"To be one of them, maybe," he replied.

"Cono Morin, go get Leader for me. Tell him it is important and to come back as soon as possible," Principal Zarena demanded.

In what seemed like a blink of an eye, Cono Morin left and came back with Leader.

"How long have the children been missing, Pilla?" he said.

"I guess no more than ten minutes," she replied.

"It had to be longer than that, because their trail is faint," he said as he looked up and pointed towards the sky, "and it is no longer day."

"Curse them! Cono Morin, break this time bubble off of us," she said. "How could we have missed it? I did not know a Traveler could travel in and out of a time bubble."

"If one does not know it is there, then one cannot break from out of it. It is reality at a slower or faster pace," Cono Morin said, breaking the bubble to the sound of the school bell chiming 9 o'clock in the evening.

"What? It has been nearly eight hours," Cona La'Sia said, "Cono Morin, how did you not sense that we were in a time bubble?"

"My dear, I did not realize it until I went to get Leader. Place your anger where it belongs; that place is not on me," he said as he turned his back on her.

"How are we going to find them, Leader?" Principal Zarena asked.

"I believe I can still track them down, but it will move much more slowly. Also, I believe we should keep the team this size. If we get a lot of people together it may cause him to act irrationally. We have some of the strongest, most talented people right here, and a proper balance: a Traveler, a Shapeshifter, and an Elementer."

"What about me?" replied Principal Zarena.

"I believe you should stay here," he said.

"Just because we are..."

"It is not that, Pilla. We must keep this as quiet as possible. It would raise suspicion if you do not go in tomorrow."

"I understand. I don't like it, but I understand," she replied.

"Ok team, let's head out," Leader said.

"How long are we going to be here?" Dar questioned examining the stone brace trapping his hands, arms, and legs against the cold, stone wall.

"That is not for me to say," Altis replied, emerging from the shadows of the dimly lit cave.

"Where did they take Grace, then?" he asked boldly.

Altis pointed up to a corner of the cave where there was a small ledge. When Dar looked up, he saw Cono Burnos bring Grace out on the cliff with a knife to her throat, "How much do you love this girl?" he yelled.

"She means the world to me, please don't hurt her!" he yelled.

"Will you pledge your loyalty to me for her life?" Cono Burnos asked.

"Dar don't!" Grace screamed. "My life is not worth you pledging to this man."

"I will," he said instantaneously. "If you let her go…you will have my loyalty to the day of my death."

"You are weak!" Burnos plunged the knife into Grace's chest causing her to let out a shallow, gargling scream. She fell to the ground as blood began to ooze out of her mouth.

"No!" Dar screamed out. "You monster! Why? Why did you kill her? She had nothing to do with this."

"She had everything to do with this when she became involved with you," he said. He plunged the knife several more times into Grace's belly and let the splattered blood drip down his cheek as he slowly removed the knife the last time.

"Stop it. She is dead!" he yelled out, "Stop it!"

"Then why does it matter if I stab her again?" he said as he slit her throat.

"Stop it! Please! I beg of you," Dar said.

"You are begging me? No son of mine should ever beg anyone," Cono Burnos said.

"What?" Dar said. Cono Burnos suddenly appeared before him with the blood-soaked knife to his neck.

"That snake of a mother of yours never told you that Dious was not your father," he replied.

"Don't talk about my mother that way," said Dar. "When I get out of here I am going to kill you."

"Now that sounds like my son," he said.

"You are not my father, and I will never be your son…Why? Why did you kill them?"

"You really would like to know, wouldn't you?" Cono Burnos replied.

"I do."

"I will not give you the satisfaction of the answer to that. Kill me, if you must, and the reasoning for my action will go down with me."

"I hate you," he spat.

"You do, don't you, but not enough," said Cono Burnos as he disappeared and reappeared with Grace's bloody body. He placed her in the center of the cave floor and started kicking her, causing dust and blood to fly in unison.

"I have killed everything that means anything to you, and I will continue to kill anyone who enters your life. Maybe I will deal with the Anakin's next, for I am done with this blind piece of trash." He gave her a swift kick in the head, causing one of her eye's to be dislodged.

At the sight, Dar fell silent. "I think that is enough…come take her away Altis."

"Yes, master," he replied as he picked up the body and walked away.

"Do you want to kill me, Dar, like I killed your mother, your father, and your friend? You want to know why I killed them?" he said as he drew closer to Dar. "Because it was fun."

Cono Burnos slowly backed away and said, "Let him go, Eres."

"Are you sure, master?" he said, slightly conflicted when he saw Dar's head was resting on his chest.

"Yes, I am sure," he replied.

Eres removed the stone braces from Dar's body, and he responded by immediately shooting a massive fireball at Altis who was re-entering the room. Altis never had a chance to scream, becoming but ash in the wind. When Dar looked up his burnt orange eyes became clouded with blackness.

"There it is. That is what I have been waiting to see," said Cono Burnos proudly.

Dar shot a massive fireball that expanded the width and length of the cave, targeted at Cono Burnos and Eres.

"What happened to him?" Eres said slowly as he barely extinguished the ball of fire. "Who is he? What is he?"

"He is what we call Jinsei," Cono Burnos replied joyfully. "Within the spectrum of life there is light and there is darkness – most people stay in the gray realm between the two extremes. Some may fall closer to the darker side, and some may fall closer to the lighter side. However, there are very few who exist solely at both extremes – those who do are called Jinsei. They rarely, if ever, exist in the in-between. They are either light or they are dark. When pushed in either direction the results are amazing, but I never thought that this would be the outcome for Dar. Isn't he beautiful?"

"We cannot control him like this," Eres said as he repelled an even stronger fireball from Dar, causing the cave to shake.

"He is not meant to be controlled. He is meant to be free to bring chaos on people," he replied.

"Was this what all the dares were for? To bring this out of him?" Eres asked as he backed away from the approaching Dar.

"Yes, yes it was," he answered gleefully. "I could not bring it out of him when I killed his parents, so I waited. Isn't he beautiful?"

"What is he?" said Eres fearfully again.

"He is perfection," said Cono Burnos.

"We have to go. Get up Leo!" Eres yelled as he approached Grace's slain body.

"The fun is over with already," Leo said, shifting from Grace's disfigured form to his own.

"Shut up, Leo!" Eres yelled.

Dar stopped and looked as Leo transformed from Grace into himself. He slowly said, "Grace?"

"This is our chance, let's go," replied Cono Burnos as he stepped into a rip, followed by Eres and Leo.

Dar stood still for a moment, looking at his hands as the ashes of Altis danced around him. Tears ran down his face as he fell on his knees murmuring, "What have I done?"

"How are we supposed to find the kids? This place is huge," Cona La'Sia said as she stepped out of the rip looking at the numerous caves embedded in the mountain. Sweeping her eyes over the massive landscape in a ferocious effort, she observed that no single entrance was alike. Each one was uniquely formed by jagged rocks and foliage around it.

Looking at her racing eyes Cono Morin said, "It won't be too hard, La'Sia. We have Leader."

Professor Lynos looked over at Leader and said, "Is something wrong?"

Leader stared in the direction of an entrance shaded by trees and said, "I smell death."

"Who has died?" replied Cona La'Sia frantically.

"Dar," he said as he walked towards the cave opening.

Hearing Leader's words, Cona La'Sia fell in silent disbelief. 'It can't be true. Maybe he is just hurt and he smells his blood,' she said to herself.

"Stay with her, Cono Morin," Professor Lynos said as he ran after Leader. When they entered the cave, sitting on the rocky ground was Dar.

"I thought you said he died," Professor Lynos said quietly.

"A part of him has," replied Leader.

"Dar – Dar is everything ok?" said Professor Lynos as he drew closer.
With his back towards them, Dar yelled, "Don't come near me!"

"What is the matter?" questioned Professor Lynos as he touched him on his shoulder.

When he turned around they noticed that one of Dar's eyes were completely black, while the other was the normal burnt orange color.

"Oh….Dar what has happened to you?" asked Professor Lynos. Hearing his sympathetic words, Dar sorrowfully told them all that happened, what they did to Grace, and what he did to them.

"How did it make you feel, Dar?" Leader questioned.

"Leader," Professor Lynos rebuked him.

"How did it make you feel, Dar?" Leader questioned again.

"I felt angry. I never felt that much anger before in my life," Dar responded.

"No, that is not what I am asking you. How did the extra strength make you feel?" Leader clarified.

"It felt powerful," he said as he clutched his fist.

"And such power has come with a heavy price," Leader said as he bent down to touch Dar's left eye.

"What has happened to my left eye?" Dar asked touching his face.

"It is pitch black. You cannot even see the white of your eye," replied Professor Lynos.

"Can you still see out of that eye?" Leader asked.

"Yes, I can."

"I see. So that side of your Jinsei has finally emerged," replied Leader.

"What? Dar's a Jinsei?" said Professor Lynos as he quickly looked at Dar. "I thought there were no more in the realm of Geo."

"What is a Jinsei?" replied Dar.

"I will tell you later. We have to go get Grace – she is not too far from here," Leader said as he walked towards an opening in the wall.

"I will go tell the others the news," Professor Lynos yelled to Leader as he ran to the cave entrance. When Professor Lynos left the cave, Dar ran after Leader.

"Please, Leader, tell me what a Jinsei is? How do I get rid of it?"

"It is nothing you can get rid of. It is like telling the sun to get rid of it brightness. This is just who you are."

"Was my father a Jinsei?"

"No, he was not."

"Was my mother a Jinsei?" he quickly uttered.

"No, she was not."

"Then how do you become a Jinsei?"

"No one really knows."

"How did Cono Burnos know that I was a Jinsei when I did not know I was a Jinsei?"

Leader sighed as he turned to Dar. "When Jinsei babies are born their hair is pure white for the first week of their life. Your mother hid you well from the public, because she did not want anyone to abuse your giftings. But your father was a talker…maybe he told Tilo the details of your birth. I really do not know. All I know is that your father told me of your hair color, so I knew. He was not worried that you would do anything bad with this gift.

"This curse," Dar corrected.

"No, it is a gift," said Leader.

"Leader, Cono Burnos said that he was my father, and when Grace and I went back in time I saw him kill my parents. He said that he could not bring the Jinsei out of me by killing my parents and that is why he killed – pretended to kill – Grace," he said.

Leader laughed. "What is so funny Leader?" Dar questioned.

"Because Tilo is not your father, be assured of that. He would say and do anything to get you upset," Leader said as he touched Dar on the shoulder. "Be assured that Dious and Aurora are your biological parents."

"I hate being a Jinsei. It caused me to kill Altis," he said.

"That is where you are wrong. You caused yourself to kill Altis," Leader replied.

"What are you saying? I am a murderer?" he said.

"That is not what I am saying."

"Stop playing games with me Leader, and tell me what I am," demanded Dar.

"You are Jinsei," replied Leader, "one who can dance between light and darkness."

"More riddles Leader?"

"No, more of the truth," he said. "Jinsei means life. Life shapes us into who we become. Many bad situations can cause some people to lean more to the darker side of life just as many good situations can cause some people to lean more to the brighter side of life. Most people never touch the extremes of life, they exist in the gray space that is between. However, Jinsei exist only, if not mostly, at the extremes. They are very light or they are very dark."

"So I jumped to the extreme when I killed Altis. I became very dark," he said softly.

"Yes, you did. You said earlier that the Jinsei in you caused you to kill Altis. You killed Altis because you wanted to. If you did not want to, you would not have. The dark side of you wanted to kill Altis. Everyone in life, whether they are Jinsei or not, has the choice to do the right thing or do the wrong thing. It does not always feel right doing the right thing, but it sometimes feels good doing the bad things. You tasted how it felt doing the bad thing. How did it feel?"

"Good at that moment, but I felt bad afterwards," he said.

"I want you to remember how it felt afterwards, because if you keep on diving into your Raygeff Jinsei – your dark Jinsei – then you will become numb to the bad things you do and you will be lost. Then your Elos Jinsei – your light Jinsei – will be lost to darkness. Do you understand?"

"I understand Leader," Dar said as he looked up to the cave ceiling. "I never told anyone this before and you must promise not to tell anyone what I am about to tell you."

"I promise," replied Leader, "as long as it will not bring harm to someone."

"Fair enough. Grace, when she looks at me, she says that she sees a sphere of light. What is that?"

"She may see your Jinsei soul, Dar."

"Do you know how she can see my 'Jinsei soul'?"

"No, I do not. The very existence of a Jinsei, as I told you before, is a mystery," Leader said as he came to a sudden stop,

"Ah…here we are. Your friend is behind this wall," he said tapping on the cold stones.

Dar placed his ear against the cold, wet stone and could hear Grace crying. "Grace, Grace….can you hear us?!" he yelled.

"Yes I can!" she replied.

"I am going to get you out of there. Stand back," he said as he used his Elementer ability to bring the wall crumbling down.

"Grace," Dar said with open arms, but she stood there and looked at him strangely.

"Grace, what is the matter?" he asked as he lowered his arms.

"Oh…it's nothing. I am just happy to see you…in a sense," she said as she walked towards him.

"Come on the others are waiting outside," Leader said.

Dar grabbed her by the hand and guided her over the rubble. When they came to the entrance of the cave, Cona La'Sia ran up to Leader and slapped him across his muzzle.

"I thought you said he was dead," she said angrily.

"I am sorry," he said rubbing his face. "I did not lie," he murmured under his breath.

Cona La'Sia then turned to Dar and said, "I made this eye patch for you. You can wear it until we figure out a way to help you."

"Thank you Cona La'Sia," he said as he placed the patch over his left eye.

"Are you okay, Grace?" Cona La'Sia asked.

"I am. But I think I am getting used to being kidnapped at this point," she said with a shallow laugh.

"That is not very funny Grace," she said.

"I know. I'm sorry," she said as she looked back at Dar.

"Okay guys and gals, let's get back," ordered Cono Morin as he created a rip leading back to Geo.

"Aren't we going to take Grace home?" Dar questioned.

"It is not safe for her to go back yet," replied Leader.

"It's no problem, Dar," Grace said, "I can spend a little bit more time in Geo."

"Cono Morin, I need you to close that rip and open one to the North Mountain village, but I need you to create it about two miles outside of the village," Leader said.

"Why?" he questioned.

"Because it is no longer safe to go back to the school. If we bring Dar back to the campus we are going to put the other students in danger," Leader said as Cono Morin closed the rip.

"So none of us can go back," said Cona La'Sia.

"That is correct," Leader announced. "We will not have to worry about Eres or Leo going back to the campus either."

"So we are going to hide?" said Professor Lynos. "What about my classes, my students?"

"We need you here. I will send a messenger bird to Pilla to tell her the situation," Leader said as he nodded towards Cono Morin who then created a rip. When they stepped through the rip and arrived at the North Mountain Village everyone gasped at the beauty of the surroundings.

"I have never seen rainbow falls before. I have heard of them, but never seen them before," Cona La'Sia said in awe. "They really are the colors of the rainbow."

"Some people are afraid to drink the water because of its color, but it is safe," Leader said smiling.

"This is so beautiful," Cona La'Sia said.

"It smells delightful. Like strawberries," Grace said letting go of Dar's hand, but he quickly grabbed it back again.

"It is that time of the year when the luka berries are collected," Leader said while looking around.

"What is the matter Leader?" replied Dar.

"We are a little further out than I wanted us to be. We have a lot of walking to do."

"How far out are we?" questioned Professor Lynos.

"About fifteen miles further then I wanted us to be."

"Well, traveling is not exact," Cono Morin said while crossing his arms with his nose in the air. "At least I got us all here, right."

"Come, my home is this way," Leader said beckoning them to follow him. "I live near the violet falls over against that cliff side. My home is the only one out there, so the village is safe if something happens."

"If something happens?" Dar said.

"Yes, that is correct," Leader replied.

"It looks like an awfully long walk," Cona La'Sia said looking down at her feet. "Can't we jump to that point?'

"No, because I do not want Tilo to track us that easily," Leader said. "Come we must move fast. They will be following us shortly."

Cona La'Sia sighed as she got off the ground and followed the crowd. As they walked down the winding roads they looked at all the strange creatures that lived at the mountain area and took in all the different smells. After about seven miles of walking down the trail, Leader guided them off into the woods where they had to cross over rivers and mud pits until they reached the Great Gap.

"You have got to be kidding me," Cona La'Sia said looking down into the chasm. "How are we supposed to go over this?"

"By faith," Leader said.

"How is faith supposed to get us across this?" she said.

"Trust me, take a step right here," he said.

"I am going to fall if I do."

"Sometimes faith requires us to take that first step into the unknown. When it seems that we are going to fall, we find out that there is a foundation keeping us up," he said as he took Cona La'Sia by the hand.

"Go on, my home is but a three mile trip down the road once we cross," he said letting go of her hand, "but never stop moving until you reach the other side."

Cona La'Sia took several steps off the cliff to discover that with every step that she took, a gust of wind came under her feet. She giggled with joy when she noticed that the wind under her feet felt like solid ground.

"How?" Professor Lynos said in amazement.

"No one knows. It is just another mystery of this great world we live in," he said as he started to walk across the Great Gap with Dar taking up the last position.

When they arrived at Leader's home their mouths dropped in awe. It was, from the roof to the very foundation, made out of camouflage stone.

"Do you sometimes lose your home?" Dar asked, looking at the forest-like home.

"No, I have never lost my home. That big red door helps me to always find it," he said pointing to the door in the distance.

When they entered his home Leader announced that Dar and Grace would have the upper room to the left, while Cona La'Sia would have the upper room to the right. He noted that Professor Lynos and Cono Morin would be sharing the lower room in the basement.

"Great," Cono Morin said sarcastically.

"And how about you, Leader?" Cona La'Sia questioned.

"I will stand guard outside," he replied.

"But you do not know how long we are going to be here," she said.

"It is my job to protect and help. A little discomfort does not bother me at all. And besides, I don't think you all will be here for long."

When Leader left, Cona La'Sia turned to Dar and Grace and pointed to the stairs, "Well, get to bed you two. It is late."

Sleepy-eyed, they both nodded their heads, then Dar guided Grace up the spiraling bronze staircase. When they reached the room, Dar saw that there were two beds positioned across from one another with a single window above each one.

When he showed Grace to her bed he sat down next to her and said, "This is not much of a room, but at least we have a bed to sleep on."

"The room really does not matter to me. I am just happy that you are near me, Dar," she said as she turned and gave him a kiss on the cheek.

"I am so glad you are safe Grace," he confided when he regained the ability to speak.

"You aren't the only one," she said as she leaned her head on his shoulder. She paused, and then blurted out, "Were you hurt while trying to save me Dar?"

"No, not really," he said looking at his arms and legs.

"Are you sure?" she said as she sat up and gave him a strange look again.

"What are you getting at Grace?" he said looking into her ice blue eyes.

"Your light – your light is cut in half," she said. "One side is the normal light that I see, but the other side is different."

"Oh…I see," he said as he lowered his head.

"What happened?" she asked with great sympathy.

"I-I killed Altis," he stammered.

"Oh, Dar… I had no idea. Were you ever going to tell me?"

"No, because I did not want you to think badly of me, to think that I am a monster."

Grace placed her forehead against his and whispered, "Dar I can never think badly of you. And you are not a monster."

He gently cupped her face into his hands, with his forehead against hers, and whispered, "It's late. I think you should go to bed."

She nodded her head. "Dar, you need to forgive yourself, or else it will eat you up and rot you to the core."

Dar stood up. "I don't think I can. Goodnight."

As the night grew longer, Dar could hear Grace whispering to someone. He turned over on his side and faced in her direction as he heard:

"Jesus, a lot has happened to me while in this place and thank you for always protecting me while I am here. My prayer tonight is for Dar. I like him a lot, but he is having a hard time right now with forgiveness. Please help him forgive and get rid of bitterness. Amen."

"Dar – Dar wake up," Leader whispered.

"What- What time is it?" he said as he rubbed his eyes realizing he had fallen asleep to Grace's words.

"Let's go," he said.

Dar crawled out of bed and walked out the room, "What is it Leader? What time is it?"

"It is very late or very earlier depending on how you look at it," he said as he descended the bronze stairway ahead of Dar.

"It is too early for these riddles, Leader," Dar said, continuing to rub his eyes.

"It is never too early for a riddle," he said.

As Dar followed Leader out of the house he said, "Where did you get that eye patch from?"

"Don't you remember that Cona La'Sia gave it to me when we came out of the cave?" he replied.

"Ohhh…yes. I remember now. I was just curious on how she made it," he said as he moved further and further into the woods.

"How far in the woods are we going to go?" Dar asked.

"Only a little further. You see where the light is coming from? We are going over there," he said, pointing to a flickering light in the distance.

"Tell me Leader, what do you see when you look up at the stars?" Dar questioned him.

"Well, I see the galaxy and all of its wonders," he replied.

As they approached the light, Dar discovered it to be a small camp fire in the middle of the woods. The moths were dancing around the flames as Leader walked closer and closer to the fire.

When he came to a stop, Dar cried out, "Cono Burnos come out and face me! I know you are here!"

A voice rang back, "And you came out here all by yourself boy."

"I did. Reveal yourself."

"How did you know, Dar Augustus?" he said as he emerged from the shadows of the woods.

"Leo here did not answer my question correctly," he said as Leo shifted back into his body.

"And you still came out here all alone," he probed.

"I did, because I can take you all on by myself," he replied.

"Do you think that you can control your Jinsei nature just after experiencing it one time?" Cono Burnos inquired.

"I can beat you without my Jinsei."

"What do you mean without? How can you be without something that is who you are? You truly don't understand yourself – what it means to be Jinsei. It is not something you tap into, it is who you are. You are a fool. Take off that patch, for I know what is underneath it."

Dar slowly reached up and moved his patch revealing his black eye.

"You are beautiful. I knew you were special when I came to your home fifteen years ago. I had traveled to so many places that day and I got lost. I found myself at the front door of your house looking for directions. I knocked and no one answered. But I heard humming around the back. It was your mother; she was giving you a bath in the backyard. Your hair was so white. I knew what you were the moment I saw you, and I desired to have your power as my own. Hoping that if I caught you as a child I could control you…" he said laughing, "…on that very day I saw right before my eyes your hair starting to turn brown. Your mother was so happy when it happened. Your mother was lovely to look at. It was a pity that I had to kill her. I left you that day and she never knew that I was there. I then met and be-friended your father and waited for my time. I planned for years how to bring forth your Raygeff Jinsei. I did small things which you probably don't remember, but nothing worked. Even when I killed your parents you did not change. But that girl – that girl made you change. Now how do you think you are going to beat me? Where do you think you stand now Dar? Are you Raygeff Jinsei or Elos Jinsei?"

"He is what he chose to be," Leader said as he came from the woods. "Do you think your time bubble will work on me Tilo? I know you. How could you betray Dious?"

"I did not care about Dious. I only cared about his son," he said pointing to Dar.

"Dious was your friend, how could you?"

"Power means more to me then friendship."

"You are such a fool," Leader said.

"Get him Leo," Cono Burnos demanded.

"My pleasure," Leo said, transforming into a dragon and charging at Leader.

"I have this Leader," Cona La'Sia said as she ran out of the woods towards Leo.

Stopping short of him, she turned to Cono Burnos and said, "I guess I should have gone with my first impression of you," she grimaced at him before turning her focus back to Leo.

"Well, Cona La'Sia, I have never hit a teacher before, but I think I can get used to it," he said.

"And I have never hit a student before, but I think I will get used to it," she said as she hit him with her newly-shifted dragon tail as she morphed.

"Dar, come join me," Cono Burnos said.

"Never!" he yelled back.

"Dar remember to control how you feel. Don't lose yourself," Leader pleaded.

"Eres, get Leader," Cono Burnos ordered.

"Yes, cono," Eres said. He picked up Leader with a whirl wind and threw him into the adjacent woods.

"I did not teach you to use your ability like that, Eres," Professor Lynos said, as he ran out of the woods.

"You did not teach me anything, Father," Eres said.

"What? He is your son?" Dar said, looking at Professor Lynos with wide eyes.

"I kept your antics to myself, to keep you out of trouble," professor Lynos said to his son, "but you have gone too far." He then turn to Dar and said, "I am truly sorry Dar, I should have done something earlier. I failed you as a teacher and as one who knew your parents."

Turning to make eye contact with his son once again he said, "What did he say that could have turned you like this?"

"He offered me power. He supported my dreams, but most importantly he spent time with me when you did not," Eres bellowed as he ran towards his father raining fireballs on him.

"I offered you my world. What else did you want?" Professor Lynos mustered with each block.

"I wanted your time. I wanted your compassion. I wanted you…But all I want from you now is to be dead."

"What else?" Dar said to Cono Burnos. "Your servants are battling with others, and now it is me and you."

"Not quite yet," he said as he created a rip. "Does he look familiar?" Cono Burnos taunted, bringing forth the creature that killed his parents.

"He will destroy us all," Dar yelled out fearfully.

"He will only destroy who I tell him to. He is under my control and… I want you to kill that one," Cono Burnos said to the beast as he pointed past Dar to a shadowy figure in the woods.

When Dar turned around he saw Grace. "No, Grace! Run!"

The beast leapt over him and charged after Grace. She got up and ran as fast as she could from the roar of the beast. As she was running she felt a hand over hers and saw Dar's crimson light.

"Run Grace, as fast as you can, I will guide you," he said.

"I am just slowing you down," she said.

"No, you are not. Stop talking, you're losing breath," he said.

"Just let me go," she pleaded as she slipped her hand out of his and fell to the ground.

"Grace, no!" he yelled as he remembered the cries of the traveler who sacrificed his life.

Swiftly, the beast leapt into the air and landed on the spot where Grace fell. Dar let out a huge yell that resonated through the woods as he charged at the beast, forming stone arms around his own. When he caught up with the monster mercy was a distant word when he could not see any part of Grace's body. Dar disassembled the beast with cruel accuracy. The beast cried out in anguish only to be silenced by decapitation.

Dar walked back to the camp and dragged the head of the beast on the ground, leaving a trail of blood behind him. When he reached Cono Burnos he threw the beast's head at his feet. He looked at Cono Burnos with his blackened eyes and said in an ominous voice, "Now it is your turn."

Dar pulled the water out of the trees and created spears with them which he threw at Cono Burnos. Burnos in turn dodged them by jumping in and out of rips. Dar created quicksand under his feet to bury him alive, but Cono Burnos was too swift for him.

"Is that all you got?" he said.

"No," he said darkly as he locked Cono Burnos' arms in place.

"How – How are you doing this?" Cono Burnos stammered.

"Did you know that the body is mostly made up of water — every muscle, every cell, almost everything?" he said as he manipulated his arm and broke it.

Crying out in pain Tilo managed a smile through the twisted agony his face was showing. Annoyed by this smile Dar questioned his expression.

In a distressed voice he said, "Look at what you have become…you are beautiful," Cono Burnos said as he spit blood out of his mouth when Dar manipulated the muscles in his leg. Twisting it around until the bones in his legs could be seen emerging through the tissues, Dar watched as that smile began to fade with each turn.

"I want you to suffer," Dar said.

"No, you don't Dar. Don't let the Raygeff Jinsei side of you win. Fight," Leader said as he limped towards him.

"I have nothing left to fight for," he said.

"Yes, you do," Grace said as she stepped through a rip, followed by Cono Morin.

"That was sure a close one with that monster jumping all over the place," Cono Morin said lightheartedly. "I had to open and close that rip so fast. I'm good."

In a dark voice, Dar said slowly, "Grace, you are alive."

"Yes, I am," she said, "but look at you."

"Both of your eyes are blackened," Leader said as he drew closer to him. "Your soul is blackened."

"Then my work is done," Cono Burnos mumbled as Cona La'Sia dropped Leo next to him on the ground.

"We have trained our students well, but not well enough," she said.

"You are correct Cona La'Sia," Professor Lynos said as he brought Eres along, encased in an air bubble.

"So now what do we do?" questioned Cono Morin.

Suddenly Cono Burnos with the use of his remaining arm created rips all about him, letting vile beasts get through. "You all die."

"Stop it Tilo. What will this prove?" Cona La'Sia cried out.

"You'll die also," Leader yelled out to him. "You only have one arm to defend yourself."

"So be it," he said, "I welcome death."

Leader barked, "Cono Morin, close these rips and look after Grace!" He then turned to Dar and yelled, "Break his other arm so that he cannot create anymore rips."

"I can't harm him. I don't want to lose myself," Dar said as he clutched his own body.

"This is not the time for this Dar. You were so willing to kill him before, and all I ask you to do is break his arm." Leader then demanded of Professor Lynos to break Tilo's remaining arm.

"Done," Professor Lynos said as he caused the ground around Burnos' arm to crush it.

Dar covered his ears at Cono Burnos' screams of pain. When he looked up he saw a beast standing over Cono Burnos. Dar looked into the man's eyes and saw something that he had never seen before – fear.

Pushing down the urge to leave him to die, Dar got up and protected Cono Burnos from the beast. With every beast he protected Cono Burnos from, Grace could see a small part of Dar's white light emerge from the crimson light. The light continued to grow as Cono Burnos grew safer.

Cono Morin closed the rip behind every slain beast, while opening a rip to remove the dead bodies. When all of the beasts were removed Cona La'Sia fell on her back deeply breathing, "Is that the last one?"

"I am too old for this," Professor Lynos said. He fell to the ground in exhaustion while looking at his son in the air bubble.

Words were soon replaced with deep breathing, then a soft voice broke the silence. "Why did you protect me?" Cono Burnos said to Dar.

"I did you wrong by damaging your body, but you did me worse. Revenge was not the answer. I can go on hating you for all my life – what would that profit me? I am choosing the path of forgiveness – I don't want my light to go into darkness. I truly hate you, but I will walk this path…Why are you laughing?"

"Because I can see that you are telling the truth. After all that I have done to you, you forgive me. Get away from me Dar Augustus, with those burnt orange eyes," Cono Burnos said as he turned his face away from Dar.

Dar touched his face and said, "Is it true? Have my eyes turned back?"

"Yes, they have. By protecting Tilo your Elos Jinsei took over," Professor Lynos said.

"And your light is brighter than ever," Grace said as she ran over to him.

Dar looked around, "Where did Leo go?"

"That coward ran into the woods during the battle," Cona La'Sia said, pointing in the direction of his escape.

"What are we going to do with Eres and Cono Burnos?" Dar asked.

"I think…" Leader was saying when Cono Burnos and Eres were pulled into a traveler's rip.

"Where did they go?" Cona La'Sia yelled.

Cono Morin opened a rip behind them, but could not see their residue path, "They are gone."

"So be it. The battle is won." Professor Lynos said as he stood up.

"But not the war," Leader murmured as he looked at Dar.

"Let's go home," Dar sighed.

"Sounds good to me," Cona La'Sia said as she came over to give Grace a hug.

Chapter Sixteen

Home?

Walking towards the back garden she saw Dar's light pacing back and forth. She could hear that he was mumbling something to himself, but could not clearly make out the words. As she approached him, she heard him stop speaking.

"What are you doing out here?" she questioned him as she took a seat on the bench.

"Trying to figure out a way to say goodbye," Dar said taking his position next to her.

"I love this garden…it is my favorite place in all of Geo. When I am gone, sit here and remember me."

"I don't want to remember you, I want you here," he said as he took her into his arms.

She gently pushed him back and placed her hand over his heart. "You will always have me here and I will always have you here," she said, placing his hand over her heart.

"Grace…" he started to say when Grace shushed him.

"It is time for me to go," she said taking his hand and standing up as they walked together to the front of the house where everyone was waiting for them.

"Are you ready to go home?" Cono Morin said.

"I am."

"Well, let's go. When you go back, time would still have moved without you. It is too difficult to try to return you at the moment you initially disappeared, so you will have a lot of explaining to do," he said.

He then turned to Dar and said, "Are you ready?"

"I am."

"I am going to miss you Grace," Cona La'Sia said.

"The school will not be the same without you," Principal Zarena declared.

"Don't forget about us," Professor Lynos added

"I won't, and I will miss you all," she said as she was guided into the rip by Dar, followed by Cono Morin.

When they walked out of the other side it was noon. Grace looked around and said, "These sounds are very familiar to me, only slightly different."

"You have an hour," Cono Morin said.

"An hour for what?" questioned Dar.

"To say goodbye. Go now, I will wait here," he said sitting on the ground against a tree.

After asking Dar several questions about her surroundings, Grace realized that she was not too far from the hunter's trail. To her own amazement, once on the trail, she was still able to maneuver down the path, with only a few stumbles. However, she suddenly began to slow down as the dirt path soon merged with a pebble one, "What is the matter?" Dar asked.

"My home is over there and I don't want to see my aunt," she said.

When Dar looked up he saw a pile of rubble, "There is nothing there."

"What? There must be."

"It looks like the house was destroyed."

"Oh no. I wonder what happened to my aunt?" she wondered mournfully. "Come, we must get to Julia's."

As they walked to Julia's house, all eyes were on Grace and this strange looking boy. No one dared to approach her in fear that she was an apparition. When they reached the house, Grace knocked on the door. Mrs. Gains opened it and passed out on the floor. Julia came running into the room when she heard the thump, yelling her mother's name, until she saw Grace and was stunned to silence.

"Grace, is that you?" she said slowly as she looked up and down at the young girl in the doorway.

"It's me, Julia," she said, taking a step forward and nearly tripping over Mrs. Gains' body.

"It can't be," she said in shock and horror, "You look the same."

"Of course, I do. Why would I look different? It's only been about 5 months since I left."

"Grace," she said still holding her position on the other side of her mother, "Did you hit your head? It has been almost 13 years since you disappeared."

Looking at Dar, Dar sighed quietly, "Professor Morin."

"I can explain everything," she said quickly, "Please trust me. I am not a ghost, an angel, a demon, or a witch," she said recalling things Julia had read to her.

Fearfully and apprehensively she approached Grace as she stepped over her mother's body and beckoned them into the house, closing the door behind them.

"Can you please place my mother on the sofa over there?" she implored Dar when her third attempt at lifting her mother failed. Dar nodded his head and picked up the unconscious woman.

"My husband and son are out right now, but they will be back later and…"

"Wait? You're married?!"

"I am. I am now Mrs. Jeremiah Wilkonson."

"And your son's name?"

"His name is Matthew."

"Ohhh…Julia, time has passed," Grace pondered out loud, before giving her congratulations.

"Thank you," she said as she guided them to the living room.

"I wish I could have been there," she sighed audibly.

"You were," Julia said, "When you disappeared everyone was out looking for you. We looked up and down the woods, but we could not find you. We only found the bracelet I gave you."

"I wondered where that had gone to," she said touching her wrist.

"I wore that bracelet the day of my wedding," she paused before saying, "Wait here, I'll go get it," she said as she dashed out the room.

"So that is Julia," Dar whispered as he watched the fair skin woman leaving.

"It is, I think. Her voice is a little different now," Grace said as she heard Julia re-enter the room.

Looking at the bracelet and then at the young girl that she thought only existed in her memories, "We were sisters and I always wanted you to be at my wedding, so this was my Grace proxy," Julia said as she slowly approached her.

"I knew you were not dead Grace. I just knew it." She shakenly put the bracelet on Grace, before closing her eyes and giving her a hug allowing all doubt and fear to melt away.

"Goodness, I am sorry that I am this way," she said softly to Grace, "I am just so afraid. You should not look this young after so long."

"I would be to," Grace said finally hugging the taller, curvier woman, "I would be to."

"Here I am an old crone and you are still young," she said drying her eyes as she laughed at her own joke, before turning her attention to Dar, "Hello, my name is Julia Wilkonson. It is nice to meet you."

Dar looked at the outstretched hand of the dark-headed woman and said, "Does your arm hurt?"

"Julia, his customs are not our customs. This is Dar Augustus," Grace introduced them.

Julia withdrew her hand, sat down on a nearby chair, and said, "It is nice to meet you Dar Augustus. How did you find Grace?"

"It is more like Grace found me," he said smiling in her direction.

"I see," she said as she looked at the love in his eyes for Grace. She then spoke up and said, "Your eyes are beautiful. I have never seen someone with that color before."

"Really, I know of lots of people back in Geo with this color?"

"Geo?"

"Have an open mind about the things I am about to tell you," Grace quickly chimed in as she started to tell Julia all about her adventures and trials in the realm of Geo.

After a while Julia exclaimed, "You expect for me to believe that Grace? I would more likely believe that you found the fountain of youth," as she laughed.

"You don't believe me?" she said in amazement.

"It is very hard to believe Grace. If it were not for your appearance, I would think that these people have bewitched you," Julia said while pointing at Dar, "He could be using magic tricks you know for his powers."

"I don't know of this 'magic' that you speak of," Dar finally spoke.

"Young man, you should be ashamed of yourself for taking advantage of this blind girl like you have done with your parlor tricks," Julia said, shaking her finger at him.

"He is not lying, Julia."

"Then prove it. If he is an — what is it? An Elementer? Create fire and I will believe your story," she said.

"Done," Dar said as he threw a fireball into the fireplace across the room, then doused it with a mini rain storm, "Is that enough proof?"

She stood stunned and unnerved for a moment, then there came a knock at the door. When she walked shakenly over to the door, slowly she looked out the window to see a crowd outside.

"It is the Sheriff," she whispered back to them before she opened the door after she composed herself.

"Good afternoon Sheriff," she said.

"Good afternoon Julia," he said. "There have been some very strange rumors coming to me that Grace is back in town. Did she come here?"

Julia looked back into the room and saw Grace shaking her head no while pointing at herself and Dar. Julia turned back to the Sheriff and said, "She has not come here. Is she really back Sheriff, or is it just more rumors?"

"I am out to see if this strange one is true. Please tell me if you do see her," he said as he tilted his hat and walked away.

"I will," she said as she shut the door.

"Thank you, Julia," Grace said.

"No problem," she replied with a little worry in her voice as she looked at the crowd dispersing from her walkway.

Turning to Grace, "It is obvious that you can no longer stay here in this town, especially looking the way you do."

"I realize that," she said bitterly.

"What's wrong Grace?"

"I came back for so many reasons, all of which don't exist anymore. My aunt's house is gone, so I haven't a home; you have aged into a wonderful woman and moved on with your life; the town and things around here are changing; the people…"

"Grace from your story," Julia interrupted, "It seems as though you have all the things you are saying you lost. As sad as I am to say this, but you no longer fit in this world."

Taking Grace by the hand she said slowly, "Grace, you will always be my sister, regardless of where you are at, but it is clear that this is not the place for you. I am going to miss you, but you have to live your new life," Julia concluded.

Speaking up again Dar said, "She is right. I and the others will be there for you."

"Go. I will tell everyone that I saw you, but once you discovered that your aunt had moved, you moved on with your new family."

"My aunt moved?"

"Yes, a few years ago a bad storm came in and knocked her house and a few other houses over," she explained, "Your aunt did not feel like rebuilding, so she moved when she got married."

"Married? Who would of thought that Aunt Gertrude would get married?"

Watching Grace taking in her story, she then turned to Dar and said, "Take good care of her."

"Always have," he said taking Grace by the hand causing her to break out of her thoughtful trance.

Julia then pulled her away and allowed her own youthful spirit to seep to the surface, "And I thought you said you will never love. He is very handsome. I am going to miss you Grace." She then spoke up and said, "Oh…I have something for you," reaching onto the bookshelf behind her.

"Here take this," she said handing her a book.

"What is it?"

"It is the story that we never got to finish. I want you to have it."

"But I can't read it."

"Maybe Cono Morin can translate it when we get back," Dar suggested.

"Thank you, Julia."

"No problem. But I think you should be going. I hear that my mother is coming to…"

Taking them around to the back of the house, Julia instructed them to take the back road, so as not to meet too many people on their journey back to the woods.

As they left, Julia waved goodbye and cried as she did many years before as she watched her dearly beloved friend and sister disappear again.

When they came back, Cono Morin was fast asleep on the ground. Dar came over and rocked him until he woke up.

With sleepy eyes he said, "I knew you were going to come back."

"Because you placed her about 13 years into this realm's future," Dar bluntly replied.

"Dar, this would have been the outcome regardless of any point and time I placed her."

"How would you know?" she questioned.

"Because when you finally find a home, it is not easy to walk away from it, no matter how tempting the past may look," he answered as he created a rip and guided the youths through it.

When they came through the rip Cona La'Sia stood up from the doorstep, walked over to Grace, and said, "Welcome home."

"Let's start the preparations," the principal said as she crossed her arms in the doorway.

"Eres," a deep voice uttered, "Tilo has failed me. Will you take his place?"

"Yes, my lord," Eres said as he bowed down to the dark figure and then departed.

"I can do better my lord. Give me one more chance. I can get him!" Tilo cried out to the dark figure.

"Your time is through," the figure said, as he consumed Tilo's body with fire.

The End

www.ingramcontent.com/pod-product-compliance
Lightning Source LLC
Chambersburg PA
CBHW070801120726
47910CB00001B/249